I0723298

AUTHOR'S NOTE

Shiraz Jones Marine Rescue Mysteries are set in England and written by an English author.

England is a country with hundreds of years of history, much of it violent. Battles and skirmishes have dotted the landscape for centuries.

As a result, when you're in England, you're never more than a few metres from a ghost.

WoooOOOooo...

6

A SPOOK IN THE DARK AT ALNCHURCH PARK

Shiraz Jones Marine Rescue Mysteries
Book Five

*Dedicated to the Reverend John Woodman,
a country gentleman.*

Copyright

A Spook in the Dark at Alnchurch Park:
Shiraz Jones Marine Rescue Mysteries Book Five

ISBN: 978-1-7636301-1-6
Imprint: The Cozy Cabin Press
10 9 8 7 6 5 4 3 2 1

CONTENTS

CHAPTER ONE

The Reverend John Woodman had owned his moped since his theological college days, so it was twenty years younger than him, which made it forty-three. At the time it was built, engines weren't as reliable as they are now, and the manufacturers had helpfully provided an alternative. John, being a forgetful man, had frequently been glad of the pedals which allowed the rider to propel the vehicle manually should it run out of petrol.

The downside was the moped was heavy and only practical to pedal on a downward slope, or, in emergencies, on the flat.

Not uphill, which was the task that faced John Woodman tonight.

Following evening bible study with his colleagues Sister Florrie and Sister Marie, Reverend John had left Redcliff vicarage replete with Bristol Cream sherry and home-made fruit cake. The sheer number of currants Sister Marie incorporated in her baking, and the faint hint of rum, persuaded John to finish a third slice before mounting his steed to return to his own parish of Alnchurch.

At the top of the shortcut via Windmill Hill Lane, overlooking the ruins of Alnchurch Park, the moped gave its all-too-familiar splutter, and its headlight extinguished. John realised, while he had taken care to refuel himself before leaving Redcliff, he had omitted to refuel the moped, and he would need to glide down the hedgerow-lined lane to the valley below. If he could just build up enough speed on the downward leg, the momentum should carry his portly frame at least halfway up the opposite side.

John paused at the crest and stared into the valley, steeling himself for the task ahead of him. He wasn't a fit man, and the less he had to pedal the unwieldy machine, the better. Stars twinkled above him on this May evening, and John realised that if he rode too fast down the steep slope and fell off the moped, help might not arrive on the remote back road until the morning. He needed to take a fine line between too much speed and too little.

Behind him, the derelict windmill which gave the hill its name creaked rhythmically. Although its sails had long since disintegrated through neglect, it still rotated slowly, even in the lightest of breezes, and the squeak of its unmaintained cogs accompanied the rustle of the trees.

Reverend John took a deep breath, glanced into the dip below and pushed off with his feet.

The moped picked up speed, and he applied the brakes gently, then released them. The downhill drift became faster, and John, fortified with the bravado of the four glasses of Bristol Cream, grinned as he aimed at the opposite slope. Once he'd made it past the valley bottom, every yard further forward meant one less yard pushing the elderly contraption.

And then—disaster. At the bottom of the hill, by the tumbledown wall and gates leading to Alnchurch Park, John's front wheel struck a stone. He wobbled sideways, failed to correct his balance and fell onto the verge.

John pushed himself to his knees, then to his feet. He wasn't injured as the grass was soft, but he was annoyed. Annoyed because now he'd have to push the machine all the way up the hill out of the valley with none of the momentum of the downhill journey to help.

He paused and stared at the task ahead of him. A full moon appeared from behind a cloud, accompanied by a gust of wind which had found its way into the valley. The windmill creaked from its position at the top of the hill, then John froze and turned his head.

An unfamiliar noise.

Not the windmill, and not the wind.

Footsteps?

John turned slowly and peered. The rhythmic crunch of gravel indicated someone was approaching.

Moonlight lit the road behind him, but he saw no one.

The footsteps scrunch-scrunch-scrunched as the invisible figure marched in a constant circuit around him.

He stared, open-mouthed, at the empty lane.

Reverend John crossed himself, abandoned his fallen moped and did something he hadn't done in over forty years.

He ran.

CHAPTER TWO

"This is the best party I've ever been to," said Emily as she joined me in the galley of my barge.

"Really? But there are only eight of us here."

"Exactly, Shiraz. You know me; I'm an introvert. Much happier in small groups. Eight is perfect."

I swept my eyes around my new home. Last week, my good friend Oscar, the retired police sergeant, had skippered the barge from its old moorings in Brighthaven Marina and, together with Emily acting as crew, we'd sailed her around to her new location in Redcliff Harbour. She lay tied to the south wall, a coveted berth where vessels stayed afloat even at the lowest tides.

"Shiraz." Murph beckoned me from his position leaning against my sofa. His bald head reflected the downlights fitted in the ceiling, and he scratched his fingers through his red-and-grey beard. "How did you score this spot to keep your new purchase? Moorings against the south wall are highly prized; you can come and go at any tide."

"I didn't intend to. I simply asked the harbourmaster if he had any spots free for an eighty-foot Dutch barge, and he told me this one was available."

"There is one downside," said Oscar, running his hand along a brass railing under the windows. "On the south side, if there's a gale, you may become trapped on board until it blows over. It's dangerous to walk around the harbour when spray's crashing over the wall. Or, equally, a storm could strand you in Redcliff town, and you'd be unable to return home."

"You can always stay in your old bed above the Wicked Whelk," said Emily. "If what Oscar's describing happened."

"Thank you," I said. "And you're always welcome to stay here, once I clear out the spare room."

Three members of Redcliff Marine Rescue, David, Jules and Frances, stood in a huddle next to Murph, our leader and coxswain. And the last guest was the vicar, Sister Florrie, who'd offered to bless my new home.

"Are you going to keep the barge's name?" she asked.

"I think so. 'Henjo'. It's a combination of the original captain's name and his wife's, Henrik and Johanna. I like it. And it's already painted on both sides."

"Painting," said Murph. "You'll need someone to perform maintenance. With the salt spray, she'll need a lot of love and attention."

"And I intend to give her that," I said. "I realised, when I woke this morning, she's the first home I've ever owned. Once I left my parents' house, I shared a flat with other aspiring models, then I married Monty and lived with him for twenty years, then I moved here and stayed with Emily. This barge is completely mine, and I can't wait to put my mark on her."

"Plus," said Jules, linking her arm with mine, "we won't have far to come if we need somewhere to sleep after a late Marine Rescue shout." She grinned.

"Of course," I said. "As soon as I unpack. Although she has two cabins, the spare one is currently full of everything I couldn't find a home for, including several cases of my clothes. And sixty pairs of shoes. And boxes of makeup and jewellery. I'll need some time to sort all that out."

We laughed.

"To Shiraz's new home," said Oscar, raising his glass.

"And all who sail in her," said Murph. "We should crack a bottle of Champagne against the side."

"You only do that when launching a boat," said Frances.

"And," I said, "it'd be a waste of good Champagne. Top-up anyone?"

"Could I have a beer?" asked Murph. "Champagne's not really my thing." He returned his untouched flute to the kitchen counter.

Sister Florrie held her arms wide. "I think now would be as good a time as any to ask the dear Lord for his blessing."

We all stood to face her, and the room quietened.

"Heavenly Father, whose Son shared at Nazareth the life of an earthly home, bless Shiraz's new abode. May it be filled with love and happiness, friends and companions. And bring us all at last to our home in heaven, through Jesus Christ, our Lord. Amen."

"Thank you, Sister Florrie," I said. "I've never heard a blessing of a home before. I'm not a religious person, but that gesture was special. It made me feel warm inside."

"You felt the presence of the Holy Ghost," said Sister Florrie. "He's here with us, you know."

"Talking about ghosts," said Oscar to Emily and me, "we should catch up for a chat. I've received an odd request for assistance, and I may need your help."

"Oh?" I said. "Tell me more."

Oscar shook his head. "Not now. Are you free tomorrow?"

"Could we make it Sunday?" asked Emily. "The café's open tomorrow morning, then in the afternoon I need a rest because in the evening we have Marine Rescue training."

"Yes," said Murph, overhearing the tail end of our conversation. "This month we're focussing on searching. I want to sign you both off on search patterns and search protocol, by night and by day. I hope you've studied radar and FLIR in your workbooks. If you want to pass your qualified crew certificates, you need to know how to use both."

I wasn't even sure where my workbook was following the relocation of everything from Emily's apartment above the Wicked Whelk café to my barge, and I certainly hadn't studied those sections.

Time to wing it again.

"No problem, Murph," I said. "Don't expect us to be completely proficient first time."

Murph gave me an odd look and tipped back his beer.

"Thanks for helping me clear up," I said to Emily, as we stacked plates into my dishwasher and stuffed leftover canapes into Tupperware. "And thanks so much for catering for my housewarming party. I know you said you didn't want any money, but I must give you something, so let me take you out to dinner. In fact, let me take you out to hundreds of dinners. You've been so good to me since I arrived here. Honestly, I would've fallen apart without you. You, Emily, rescued me."

"Don't say that, Shiraz. I'll start crying." She wiped her eyes. "I think I've drunk too many Champagnes. They go down so easily."

"D'you want to stay on the couch?"

"No, it's a five-minute walk home around the harbour. I'll be fine. I have to open the café in six hours. A nap tomorrow before night training will help."

"Have you studied the sections on radar and FLIR, like Murph said? I know what radar is, but I've never heard of FLIR."

"FLIR stands for Forward Looking Infra Red. It's a device used for searching for people at night. Their body heat shows as a white blob. Frances told me. I'm looking forward to testing it for real."

"Got it. I'll try to remember the acronym. I'll finish here. You go home and get to bed. It's nearly midnight. The witching hour."

"Thanks. I have a full day tomorrow, and then Oscar's popping around on Sunday. What's that all about?"

"No idea. He was very secretive. It had better not be another murder."

"Unless we find another body ourselves, which I hope we never do again, that's the last of those." Emily hugged me. "Goodnight, Shiraz. See you tomorrow. Pop in to collect your coffee. Just because you don't live with me above the café anymore doesn't mean you're allowed to be a stranger."

I closed the door behind Emily and returned to my living room. This was the first party I'd hosted since my sudden escape to Redcliff, after I'd fled my London career as the arm-candy of an unfaithful society man thirty years older than me. Back in those days, life had been one non-stop party, running from the gym to lunch with modelling friends so I could listen to them talk about mutual acquaintances behind their backs, then a quick change of outfit for an interview with a magazine editor, always accompanied by a glass or two of Bollinger. The early evening would start with another clothing selection conundrum, then off to a formal dinner where one of my husband's clients would inevitably make inappropriate remarks to me, and my husband would expect me to tolerate these. After that, maybe we'd go to a film premiere where I was required to twist and turn on the red carpet, shine my gleaming, faultless, expensive smile, and look interested in some director's remake of a 1970s horror movie. Then dash home for yet another costume change, because a girl can't be seen twice in one evening wearing the same dress, can she? Back in the Rolls to drive to an invitation-only after-party, where I had to nod, smile and never say a longer sentence than, 'Oh, how interesting,' or, 'Goodness, you're so talented.' Unfailingly, this would blur into carrying on to a nightclub, consuming a significant number of cocktails and finally collapsing into bed sometime around 3:00 a.m., ready to be up at 10:30 to grab two or three coffees and do it all over again.

I should have escaped the hamster wheel years previously and done something for me. And now I was doing exactly that. I was a marine rescue volunteer on my way to becoming a useful qualified member of the crew and not attending too many parties.

The spare room door glared accusingly at me.

What on earth am I going to do with all my outfits?

"Tonight," said Murph, as the rescue vessel steamed slowly out of Redcliff Harbour, "we'll learn how to use the radar and how to use the FLIR. Both are acronyms, although radar's become a commonly used word in its own right. Who can tell me what either stands for?"

"FLIR means Forward Looking Infra Red," I said.

Phew. I hope he thinks I've read the subject matter.

"Very good, Shiraz. You've been studying. What's it used for?"

"Searching for people at night. It sees the heat of their bodies."

"Excellent," said Murph. "How many FLIRs do we carry?"

Oh, no. Maybe each crew member has one?

"Um, four?"

"Galloping genoas, Shiraz. We're not that rich. FLIRs are expensive pieces of kit. Nope, we have two. One fixed to the vessel, and one you hold in your hand. I'll ask Frances to demonstrate them later. Next, radar. What does radar stand for?"

I crossed my fingers and hoped the fact I'd answered one question correctly meant it was someone else's turn.

"Emily?" asked Murph.

"I thought it was just called radar."

"Frances," said Murph to the qualified crew member with us. "What does radar stand for?"

"Sorry, Murph. I'm not sure that's part of the course."

"You're right, it's not."

I felt my shoulders relax.

"I just wondered if anyone knew?" said Murph. "Radar stands for Radio Detection And Ranging. It's a way for vessels to see each other at night and also to navigate around landmasses. It works by reflecting signals off nearby objects and displaying the results on a screen. We'll turn it on now and take a look. Frances, could you demonstrate to these recruits how to switch on the radar?"

"Yep. Watch over my shoulder." She pressed a menu on the navigator's screen, and a green rectangle appeared with the word 'Transmit' in the centre. "Push this button. There. Now the radar's on, and you can see the output on the screen."

I peered around her and watched as red lines and blobs formed, dancing and continually changing shape as if they were abstract projections in a trance nightclub.

Frances pointed at the various shapes. "You can see the outline of the coast, and that odd-shaped lump's Blakey's Island. The six small red dots are probably the fishing fleet heading out to deeper waters."

"What are those bits that keep appearing and disappearing around us?" I asked.

"Waves, and the boat's wake. Radar's not perfect, and we'll try to tune out some of that clutter, as it's called. The best radar reflection comes from anything metal, such as a ship."

"And the worst," said Murph, "comes from anything plastic or wooden, such as a kayak or a small rowing boat. Not that they should be out at night. And yachts can also be invisible.

Many of them carry metal radar reflectors in their rigging, so they show up on the screen. Right, that's radar. Now for the FLIR. Let's head towards Redcliff Main Beach, and I'll show you something fun."

CHAPTER THREE

Murph drove the boat towards the string of white lights which marked the sweeping promenade lining Redcliff's seafront. After dark on this mild May evening, couples strolled arm-in-arm along the walkway, and dogs cavorted next to their owners, enjoying their evening exercise on the sand.

He pushed a toggle switch down, and the anchor clattered to the bottom of the sea. We swayed gently in the waves and waited for his demonstration.

"Switch on the FLIR, Frances," he instructed.

Frances pushed a circular button with the universal power symbol on it. A small screen above showed the pattern of the swell around the rescue boat in a uniform light grey.

"Wow," I said. "It turns night into day. You can see the waves so clearly. But if I look out of the window, I can't see them at all."

"Show them what a person looks like," said Murph.

"The FLIR's on the roof of the cabin," said Frances, "and you steer it with the joystick." She wiggled a knob, and we heard a whirring sound above our heads. The image on the screen changed from rolling waves to a dazzling light, which I concluded was a streetlight on the promenade.

Frances gazed out of the window. "Okay, I'll line it up, and—there."

The picture revealed a white blob in the unmistakable shape of a person walking with a dog-shaped blob alongside them.

"See?" said Frances. "It's picking up the heat of the man and the dog. Imagine how useful that is for searching for someone in the water at night."

"Definitely," said Emily. "Have you found people for real using the FLIR?"

"Yes," said Frances. "D'you remember that job we went to last year, Murph? The chaps in the rowing boat?"

"How could I forget? We'd been called out to three men who'd fallen in the sea from an overturned vessel between Redcliff and Blakey's Island. By the time we received the shout and headed out of Redcliff Harbour, it was dark. One man in the boat had called for help and, thankfully, we had a position from his phone. Once we reached them, they'd been in the water for fifteen minutes, and they were freezing. But we only found two men, and I feared the worst. They said their friend had swum for shore, which was a terrible idea. If your boat turns over, and it's still floating, you should always remain with it, because we can find a boat much more easily than a person. Anyway, after we'd pulled the two guys on board, we began a search for their friend. Frances looked at the screen of the main FLIR, and David was using the portable one. Within five minutes, he saw the image of a man trying to swim, exhausted and chilly from staying afloat. We retrieved him, and I'd say the FLIR saved his life that night."

"Gosh," I said. "A close shave. Could we see the portable FLIR? Does it work in the same way?"

"Exactly the same, although the image quality's better on the handheld, even though it's smaller, because it's a newer model. The main FLIR needs replacing; it keeps getting stuck pointing at the sky, which would only be useful if we were searching for hang gliders. They don't make parts for it anymore, so as soon as we receive the next significant grant or donation, we'll replace it. Frances, could you pull out the portable FLIR to show them?"

Frances reached into a locker beside her and withdrew a soft, black case, which she unzipped. She tugged out an item which looked like a big, black, square lollipop, with a handle on the bottom and a screen on top. She handed it to me.

"This is a FLIR E-54," she said. "It costs over five thousand pounds, and it's one of the best handheld thermal imaging devices on the market."

"Five thousand pounds?" I sucked in a quick breath. "That's a lot of money. How much is the one on the roof which we need to replace?"

Murph grunted. "The new model is the M-364, which costs twenty thousand pounds including tax and fitting. We need a grant or a generous benefactor, and we need them now."

Frances handed me the portable FLIR. "Here. It works just like the main one. Have a try at pointing it at people on the beach, but don't aim it directly at the streetlights; you could hurt your eyes."

I turned it towards the sand. The man and the dog appeared as even clearer blobs, and I followed their path as they trotted along the beach. Then I swung it to the right and lit up two people embracing passionately behind a breakwater.

"Oops." I showed Emily and Frances the image. "Maybe I should aim in another direction?"

We all laughed.

"Right, team," said Murph. "Let's set up a sector search on the instruments, and we'll practise using these tools for real."

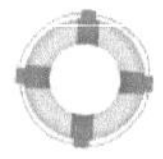

We sat around Emily's dining table the following morning, a strange combination of the familiar and the odd for me. I didn't live with her anymore, and I couldn't simply walk back into her spare bedroom to grab a hairbrush or a stick of lip gloss. Emily had rung me at 9:45, a tad early for me on a Sunday, and asked if I could please come around for breakfast as she didn't fancy eating by herself. Which suited me fine, as I realised that apart from left-over cheese-and-tomato mini quiches which were no longer at their best, stale salt-and-vinegar crisps and curled-up cucumber sandwiches, I didn't have a crumb of food on board. Boots had somehow infiltrated my home to spend the night, and when I awoke, I'd discovered the plump ginger tom snoring on my dining table surrounded by flakes of sausage roll pastry. He then followed at my heels as I walked to Emily's apartment.

"How do I arrange for Redcliff supermarket to deliver to the barge?" I asked her as I sipped my coffee. "I don't have an address, so their website won't accept my order."

"You could give them mine?" she suggested. "And collect the groceries from here."

"But what if you're out? You don't want to be waiting in for someone else's groceries. I'll have to call in to see them. Hopefully, we can work something out."

"I could collect food for you from the wholesaler?"

"That's very kind of you, Emily, but I'm not the most organised with my grocery shopping. I don't think I could give you an order for a week's worth of supplies without needing a top up each day. No, I have to work out how to receive grocery deliveries myself, and not rely on your generosity."

THUMP THUMP THUMP

"Oscar," we both said.

I jumped up to answer the door before remembering Emily should be the one doing that.

She smiled and gave me a 'go ahead' motion. I clumped down the stairs to find Oscar standing on the doorstep with Cadbury, his chocolate Labrador.

"Morning, Shiraz," he said. "I'm glad you're here at Emily's as I want to speak with both of you. Is Boots in?"

"Yes. Probably stealing bacon from my plate as we speak."

"You'd better nip back upstairs quickly." He laughed and turned to the dog. "Sorry, Cadbury. You'll have to wait here for me." He tied him to a hook in the wall outside the Wicked Whelk and stomped up the steep stairs.

"Hi, Oscar," said Emily. "Kettle's boiled. Earl Grey?"

"Yes, please. My wife's at her Sunday morning church service, so I've slipped out."

"That sounds very covert," I said. "Are you keeping a secret from her?"

"Not really. I'm omitting to tell her something. Not quite the same."

"Right." I laughed. "Do you need to tell us? At my bargewarming party, you mentioned something about a ghost. But Halloween's months away, so I wasn't sure what you meant."

"Sister Florrie spoke about the Holy Ghost, but the ghost I'm thinking of isn't religious."

Emily grinned as she placed Oscar's tea and a refill of coffee for me on the table. "Oscar, spill the beans. Stop beating around the bush."

He sighed, leant on his elbows, scratched his forehead and sucked in a breath.

We waited.

"I have a conundrum," he said, finally. "And I'm undecided who to discuss it with. I'm not sure if it's supposed to be confidential."

"Ok-ay," I said. "I'm relatively new in town, so maybe I can be a sounding board?"

"You know me, Oscar," said Emily. "I'm so shy in social situations, I hardly say anything to anyone. What's your conundrum? You must be going to tell us, otherwise you wouldn't have come around." She looked hopefully at him. "Would you?"

"I'll bite the bullet. Do either of you know, or have you heard of, a woman called Lady Dulvington?"

"Never," I said.

"I've heard the name Dulvington," said Emily. "Is it a village further along the coast?"

"Yes, but the woman called Lady Dulvington lives near Alnchurch, on a country estate eight miles out of Redcliff. She inhabits the gatehouse of her ancestral home, Alnchurch Park."

"I know where that is," said Emily. "It's the driveway you see once you've passed the derelict windmill, on the old road between here and Alnchurch. I haven't used that back lane for years since the new bypass was built. My car struggled to make it up the steep hill and, near the top, I was always terrified she'd roll backwards."

Oscar laughed. "You're right, the estate is in a deep valley. All you can see from the road is the entrance, the driveway and the gatehouse. Alnchurch Park used to be one of those vast old country mansions, but it was bombed during the war and mostly destroyed. The Dulvington family, like so many of the landed gentry, were asset-rich and cash-poor, and they didn't have the money to repair it. The house became unsafe and had to be abandoned completely as more and more masonry crumbled. It now stands as a ruin, and the last remaining member of the Dulvington family's retreated to the gatehouse."

"That's so sad," I said. "Imagine waking up every day and seeing your former home falling to bits while you live next door."

"The family could've repaired it," said Oscar, "if only Lady Dulvington's grandfather had been less stubborn. He refused to sell any of the estate's land, which would've raised the necessary funds to make the house habitable. Parts of the house date from the 1500s, and there's even a rumour Queen Elizabeth I stayed there, although that can't be substantiated. But, in the post-war days of the 1950s, Britain was a very different place to the present day, both financially and in attitudes. Buildings which had been bombed were pulled down without a second thought. Alnchurch Park mostly fell down by itself."

"So…Lady Dulvington?" said Emily.

"Yes, I'm coming to her. Many years ago, when I was the serving sergeant in Redcliff, Lady Dulvington summoned me from the police station. She wanted to speak with me, she said, as she'd had dealings with the Alnchurch police, and they hadn't impressed her. I didn't want to step on another sergeant's toes, so before I went to see her, I cleared it with him. He was quite happy for me to visit her. In fact, he said he'd prefer it if I did. Apparently, she'd somehow obtained his home phone number, and she'd ask her butler to contact him at all times of day and night, so he ended up ignoring her calls."

"Oh. So you visited her at Alnchurch Park?"

"I rang her initially, being careful to keep my home number secret. It transpired she'd been burgled, and the thieves had stolen a valuable painting. It was one of the few undamaged ones she'd retained when she retreated to the gatehouse. She was particularly distressed, as the artwork was not only painted by Thomas Gainsborough, one of Britain's most famous portrait painters, but it also depicted her great-great-grandfather. That's probably not enough greats, given Gainsborough painted during the 1700s. Regardless, the picture was of a former Lord Dulvington standing on the steps of the estate. Few photographs survive of the building in its full glory before Hitler began his demolition work, so the painting was one of the few memories she had of her childhood home."

"Was it worth a lot of money?" I asked.

"She estimated fifty thousand pounds, which would be a lot more today. And, of course, it was uninsured and possibly uninsurable."

"How distressing for her," said Emily. "Did you ever find it?"

"I did. That was a very complex case, but I had a lucky break. Lady Dulvington owned a photo of herself with the painting in the background. I enlarged the relevant part and sent a copy to a contact of mine who works at a local auction house. He circulated it around his industry, asking auctioneers to be on the lookout. The case remained open for over a year, and I endured weekly phone calls from Lady Dulvington, in some distress, pleading with me to find her picture. Then my contact called me. An art expert working at an auction house called Bonham's in London had been asked to value a collection of paintings for insurance. The owner was from Hong Kong, and he was returning to live there and taking a collection of art with him which he'd inherited from his late father. But"—Oscar held up one finger—"it seems our friend from Asia's parent had obtained some of his acquisitions by less-than-regular means. Not only was Lady Dulvington's painting discovered among his collection but also several other works of art which had been reported stolen over the years, including a Pissarro, a Caravaggio and a Renoir. The recoveries set the art world alight. Fortunately, I managed to keep my name out of the papers."

"Goodness. And your conundrum…?"

"All in good time, Shiraz; the backstory's important. Lady Dulvington was naturally overjoyed with the return of her painting, and she offered me a significant sum of money as a reward. I explained I wasn't permitted to accept it personally so, instead, she donated it to the Police benevolent fund. She invited my wife and I to tea shortly afterwards and embarrassed me terribly by heaping praise on me in front of Mrs Wainwright who is, naturally, my greatest critic."

We laughed.

"Um, so how does this tie in to the Holy Ghost?" asked Emily.

"Because, last night, I received a call on my home phone from Lady Dulvington herself."

"Oh, no," I said. "How did she get your personal number?"

"Now I'm no longer with the police, it's no secret. Between my role as acting mayor, my involvement with the Rotarians, and my membership of the Redcliff Icebergers swimming club, I'm sure anyone who looked hard enough could find it. Lady Dulvington told me she had a private matter which needed investigation and asked me to come around to discuss it.

Naturally, I replied that I'd retired over ten years ago, and I gave her the number for Redcliff police. Alnchurch police station, as you may know, doesn't exist anymore, and the patch is split between Redcliff and Headland Bay. She objected and stated she wanted to see me and nobody else, so I presumed she'd had a similar experience with the new sergeant at Redcliff as she'd formerly had with the Alnchurch police. I explained I was a private citizen who couldn't be involved in investigating crimes in any official capacity. But she wouldn't take no for an answer."

"No, no, no," said Emily, holding her face in her hands. "Please tell me you haven't signed us up for privately investigating a murder? I know we've solved cases earlier this year, but that was because Shiraz and I came across bodies, and we became semi-willing participants in the investigations. I don't want to set up some kind of back-street detective agency."

"Definitely not," I said. "I have an image of Emily and me, dressed in trench coats, creeping around Redcliff's streets with magnifying glasses."

Emily laughed. "What would we call ourselves? The Seaside Sleuths?"

Oscar grinned and shook his head. "Nothing of the kind. Nobody's died, at least not recently, so no murders need investigating."

"What d'you mean by 'not recently'?" I asked. "D'you mean a cold case, like that skeleton in the landslip? I don't want to investigate another one of those either."

Oscar sipped his tea, and I gritted my teeth as he made us wait.

"No," he said finally. "It's not a cold case. Lady Dulvington needs a sharp mind, but not from the constabulary."

"Come on, Oscar, we're bursting to know," I said.

Oscar hesitated. "Very well. Her private matter, which almost definitely isn't a crime, is this."

He paused, as if deciding whether to divulge it to us.

We waited as he inhaled and tapped his hands together.

He set his jaw and looked up at us. "Lady Dulvington has a very unusual problem. She claims she's being haunted."

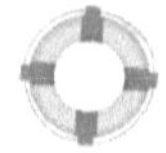

CHAPTER FOUR

"Lady Dulvington's being haunted?" I asked. "This is fascinating. I've never heard of someone being haunted, apart from in a ghost story."

"I never read ghost stories," said Emily. "I can't see why anyone would. Why take a book to bed which scares you so much, you stay awake? My friend took me to see a movie of a Stephen King book called *Pet Sematary*, and I didn't sleep for three entire nights afterwards. Never again."

"There's a perfectly natural explanation for Lady Dulvington's matter, of course," said Oscar. "Because ghosts don't exist."

"Oh, I do believe in them," said Emily. "I read a non-fiction book which explained exactly what happens when people die, and how their soul separates from their physical body."

"I thought you said ghost books scared you?" I frowned at her.

"Yes, but the book was more scientific than scary. I'm actually fascinated by the afterlife. When I die, I want to come back as a cat." She gazed at Boots, who'd found a patch of sunshine on the floor and stretched out across most of it.

"I've even heard your soul can separate from your physical body while you're still alive," I added. "Something called 'flying on the astral plane'. I had a model friend in London whose mother claimed to be a psychic; one of those ladies who never really left the 1970s. She always wore a headband and had long strings of beads dangling around her neck. She used to hypnotise people and help them have out-of-body experiences."

"Utter hogwash," said Oscar. "Smoke and mirrors, at best. There are no ghosts, no out-of-body experiences and no afterlife. When you're dead, you're dead. That's it."

"If you don't believe in the occult, Oscar, why have you agreed to help Lady Dulvington?"

"I haven't, by any means. But I am curious as to what's really going on. She told me she'd heard wailing noises coming from the ruins of Alnchurch Park after dark, and she'd seen a distant figure in white floating through the remains of the building."

"A spirit," said Emily. "I can feel the hairs on the back of my neck prickling now."

"You can call it a spirit if you like. I prefer the term, 'Mischievous teenagers.' Regardless, I'm not sure how I should respond to her. And I wondered if you two had any suggestions?"

"Did you?" I asked. "Really? Are you sure you don't have something else in mind? Because I can see a glint in those eyes of yours which betrays your intentions."

"You're very sharp, Shiraz. I can't hide anything from you, can I? All right, I'll admit it. My curiosity's piqued. I have made an appointment to visit Lady Dulvington, and I wanted to ask if you'd accompany me? Given that we've solved multiple murders together, I thought a little mystery with unexplained noises and sightings of white figures might offer a diversion."

"We don't have to catch the ghost, do we?" asked Emily. "I don't think I could sneak around an abandoned stately home at night searching for phantoms."

"Oh, I don't know," I said. "We might jump on top of a mummy, pull the bandages off its face and discover it's Mr Smithers, the janitor inside."

"Who's Mr Smithers, the janitor?" asked Oscar.

"Shiraz has been watching too much *Scooby Doo*," said Emily, grinning. "Do you really think teenagers are making the noises and apparitions, Oscar?" She grinned at me. "Rather than Mr Smithers?"

"I'm not sure if the sightings are teenagers specifically, but I am sure of one thing. There are definitely no such things as ghosts."

"I haven't driven along this road for years," said Emily. "The old windmill's become more decrepit, hasn't it? It's sad when buildings aren't maintained. History's lost."

"I don't remember the windmill in use," said Oscar, "and I've known it all my life. When I was a boy, gosh, around sixty years ago, my friends and I would come down here to pick apples from the estate orchard. The gardener at the time would permit us to keep half the crop in return for picking them. Which we thought was a good deal, as we used to eat several while we worked."

"I like that arrangement," I said.

"Yes, and it was good, old-fashioned fun, climbing through the branches and seeing who could pick the most apples. Although I fell out of the trees more than once."

We laughed at this thought, as Emily paused her Morris Minor at the top of the hill which fell away from the windmill to Alnchurch Park's driveway. The sound of birdsong accompanied the creak of the dilapidated mill's sails as they turned.

"I remember the last time I was here," she said. "The Morris Minor's brakes overheated on the way down, and the car ran halfway up the hill on the other side out of gear."

"Out of gear?' said Oscar. "Why were you running the car out of gear?"

"To save petrol. My father taught me that trick."

Oscar covered his eyes. "Let me teach you a safer one. Put the gearstick into second, and we'll crawl down gradually. The gears will help you brake."

Emily pushed the Morris's old gearstick to the left, let out the clutch, and we drifted slowly down the hill. As we picked up speed, she braked sharply, and my face collided with her headrest.

"Sometimes I wish you had seatbelts," I said, rubbing my forehead.

"Sorry. I'm terrified she'll run away with me."

Squeaks emanated from under the car as we arrived at the bottom of the hill, and Emily swung the wheel left into the driveway. A stone, single-storey building with four white-framed sash windows and a slate roof stood on the left-hand side of the drive. Despite the sunny, early summer day, the house appeared dingy and dark, and I wondered if down here in the valley it ever saw any sun.

"The gatehouse," said Oscar. "All that remains of the old Alnchurch Park."

"How old is it?" I asked.

"I reckon it dates from the late 1700s. Presumably it replaced a previous building. The gatehouse was undamaged by the bombs, which is why Lady Dulvington retreated here in the 1950s."

"Gosh," said Emily. "Poor Lady Dulvington. Imagine watching bits drop off your grand, ancestral home all around you and reducing yourself to living in what was your servants' quarters."

"You'll find she's quite stoic about her situation," said Oscar. "She must be almost ninety, and she still retains a small staff. She employs a butler, a gardener and some kind of maid, or personal assistant."

"Where was the main house?" I asked.

"Further down the drive, on the opposite side of the valley. We may be able to take a look at it after we've met her. Of course, in the old days, the purpose of whoever lived at the gatehouse was to stop you doing exactly that. Alnchurch Park is uninhabitable, on account of it missing almost all of its walls and its entire roof. But, as far as I know, you can still see the layout and get an idea of what it might've been like in its days as a country house. Not quite on the scale of *Downton Abbey*, but pretty close. I think the Redcliff and Alnchurch Historical Society may have a photo from after the war, before it collapsed completely. Anyway, park here, and we'll meet Lady Dulvington and see what she wants."

Emily stopped the car outside the gatehouse, and we climbed out.

She hesitated. "We're not actually going to see the ghost now, are we? I have a vision of us all sitting in Lady Dulvington's front room and suddenly a headless horseman rides through the wall."

Oscar rolled his eyes. "May I remind you, there are no such things as ghosts. Which is, I'm sure, why the police gave her the brush off, and she called me. We'll discover the noises and apparitions which she's reported are nothing but teenagers playing pranks." He marched up to the front door and banged the knocker three times.

"Police knock, as always," I whispered to Emily.

"I'm scared," she said. "Be ready to run if the pictures start falling off the walls."

A tall man with a long, thin face opened the door. He wore a black dinner suit and a bow tie, and white gloves adorned his hands.

"Good afternoon, sir and mesdames," he said, in a deep, slow voice. "May I help you?"

"Good afternoon," said Oscar. "We're here to see Lady Dulvington."

"Do you have an appointment?"

"We do."

"Who may I say is calling, sir?"

"Oscar Wainwright, retired police sergeant. These are my associates, Shiraz Jones and Emily Philpot."

"Very good, sir. Please wait here." He closed the door, and we stood vacantly in front of it as if we were calling to sell an insurance policy.

"Associates, Oscar?" said Emily. She grinned. "Oscar and Associates' Ghost Hunting Agency? Shall I have some business cards printed?"

"That won't be necessary. Lady Dulvington isn't expecting anyone but me, so I needed to introduce you. And 'associates' seemed to be the most appropriate word."

"Right. Associates."

The door reopened. "This way, please, sir, mesdames."

We entered through a small vestibule and turned left into a square room with a dark-green Chesterfield sofa and a matching armchair, both of which faced a fireplace. No flames burnt, but I noted the glow from one element of a three-bar electric fire placed in the hearth. It didn't warm the room to a comfortable temperature, and I shivered. A picture of a seated, unsmiling man hung above the fireplace, and I glanced back and forward between the painting and the armchair as I realised it depicted him sitting in the same piece of furniture.

"Wait here, please," said the butler. "M'lady will attend to you shortly." He reversed out of the door we'd entered and closed it.

"This room," said Oscar in a low voice, "is unchanged since my last visit forty years ago."

"It's clean, though," said Emily. She ran her finger across a polished, wooden occasional table with a half-full decanter standing on it. "There's no dust. She must employ a cleaner."

"How big is the gatehouse?" I asked. "Does the butler live here too?"

"Yes. It must have five or six rooms," said Oscar. "The living room, then on the opposite side of the front door is a dining room. Lady Dulvington and the butler must have a bedroom each. Then there would be somewhere where food is prepared, and presumably at least one set of washing facilities."

A floorboard creaked, and Emily grabbed my arm. "Was that the ghost?"

Oscar rolled his eyes. "There are no ghosts. These old houses creak and groan all the time."

"Maybe that explains the noises she heard? Case closed."

"She heard wailing," I said. "Not creaks and groans."

"Ghosts wail, don't they? They do in *Scooby Doo*."

"Emily, please," said Oscar. "There'll be a perfectly simple explanation."

"How long are we going to stand here?" I asked. "Should we cough loudly to remind her we've arrived?"

"Patience," said Oscar. "The aristocracy are accustomed to people waiting for them. Ah, I heard footsteps. I think she's coming."

A door to the rear of the room opened, and in walked the oldest supermodel I'd ever seen. With exquisitely coiffured white hair, a made-to-measure green dress styled as if she were about to attend a ball at a royal palace, and a white shawl, Lady Dulvington was the epitome of elegance. I had to stop myself staring, as her presence commanded the room. Three brown-and-white Corgis trotted at her heels, each keeping its nose upward towards her right hand. I smiled at the memory of my childhood pet, my own Corgi, Poppy.

"Sergeant Wainwright, so good of you to come," she said, popping a treat into each dog's mouth.

"My pleasure, Lady Dulvington." Oscar bowed slightly from the neck. "The sergeant title has gone with my retirement, I'm afraid, but thank you for remembering."

"Nonsense," exclaimed Lady Dulvington, distributing a scent as she turned which I recognised as *Beauty Black Opium* by Yves Saint Laurent. "If you're going to call me 'Lady', I'm happy to return the favour, Sergeant. And I trust things with the council and the Rotary club are well?"

"They are, Lady Dulvington." Oscar smiled and bowed slightly again. "These are my associates," he said, gesturing extravagantly at Emily and me. "Ms Shiraz Jones and Miss Emily Philpot."

I held out my hand to shake in the usual manner and found myself clasping Lady Dulvington's in an action which I'd last performed when I'd been presented to the Queen at The Royal Variety Show.

"Well, well, well," said Lady Dulvington, smiling at me. "Shiraz Jones. I didn't expect to meet you here today."

CHAPTER FIVE

"Shiraz Jones," said Lady Dulvington, looking me up and down. "It's been a while since you graced the front cover of *Red Carpet Superstars* magazine. I'll hazard a guess at 2010."

"Goodness," I said. "You're right. When I was at the height of my so-called career."

"And," said Lady Dulvington, "You've made the inner pages many times since. But I think you did well to break it off with Montague. He sounded like a cad."

My mouth fell open. How old had Oscar said she was? Ninety? She had no idea she'd be meeting me today, or indeed ever, and she knew all about my life.

"And Miss Philpot." Lady Dulvington permitted Emily to take her hand. "Chef extraordinaire at the Wicked Whelk, as it's now known. What an honour to have you grace my abode."

Emily's mouth formed a similar shape to mine. "Thank you," was all she managed to reply.

"Where are my manners?" continued Lady Dulvington. "Please, be seated." She sat in the high-backed, Chesterfield chair at right angles to the fire, and I noticed how nimbly she moved for a lady of her age. The Corgis arranged themselves at her feet.

"Will you take tea with me today?" she asked.

This wasn't a request, I realised, but part of the ritual.

"Thank you," said Oscar. "Tea would be welcome."

"Black Earl Grey, no sugar, isn't it, Sergeant Wainwright?"

"Yes," said Oscar. "What a memory you have."

I half-expected her to tell me my usual order was a double shot skinny latte, but we hadn't met before, and her knowledge bank, which appeared to rival Wikipedia, didn't extend to the details of my preferred beverage.

"And for Ms Jones and Miss Philpot?" she asked.

"Earl Grey would be fine, thank you," I said.

Emily nodded. "Me, too."

"Very good," said Lady Dulvington. She reached to her left and dingled a small handbell. Seconds later, the door to the hall opened, and the butler appeared. I looked him up and down and decided if I ever had a butler, I'd expect him to look exactly like this chap. In London, Monty and I survived with a cook, a cleaner and a handyman-cum-gardener, but none of them lived in.

"Yes, m'lady?"

"Earl Grey tea, Barrowman. For four. And my usual afternoon pick-me-up."

"Very good, m'lady." He reversed out of the door and closed it.

"So, Ms Jones." Lady Dulvington sat forward with her hands clasped, and I again noted how her movements reflected those of a significantly younger woman. "You've arrived in Redcliff-upon-Sea from London, leaving behind a marriage and a career amongst the glitterati to donate your time to those in danger on the sea."

I thought the meeting was supposed to be about ghosts, not me?

"I have, Lady Dulvington. You seem very well informed."

"Ms Jones, I keep my ear well to the ground. At my age, you find yourself restrained to an ever-decreasing social circle, and I like to relive my youth through the society pages."

"Lady Dulvington was a debutante," explained Oscar.

"I was," she said, "and I may have indulged in a little showing off in my younger days. Back in the 1950s, Ms Jones, I was a predecessor of yours."

"You were a model?" I inspected her more closely. Her fine cheekbones and slim, elegant build could certainly be those of a retired catwalk superstar.

"I dabbled a little in it, yes. Until my marriage."

"Is your husband still alive?" I asked.

"No. He passed away years ago. He was a heavy drinker and a career smoker. If ever I smell the brand he used to smoke, *Capstan Full Strength*, I'm immediately reminded of the hell I endured at his hands. Not that I smell smoke much these days. Nobody seems to indulge any more. The only chap I know who takes the odd puff is the gardener, Stokes."

"The gardener doesn't live on site, does he?" asked Oscar.

"No. Barrowman's the only full-time staff member remaining. He's been with the family since he was a boy. Stokes is a younger man. He comes every weekday to maintain the grounds. And then there's my daily, of course. Jennings."

"Daily?" asked Emily.

Oscar glanced at her.

"Now, now, Sergeant," said Lady Dulvington. "I can't expect Miss Philpot to understand my old-fashioned expressions. Jennings is a young lady who attends to me three days per week. She arrives around eight, serves my breakfast and helps me rise. She performs household chores until noon, when she prepares a little light luncheon before she leaves. Then she calls back in the late afternoon and reads with me before supper. That's in her own time, not part of our agreement. I honestly don't know what I'd do without her. She's very good to me, like the daughter I never had. I suppose I'll have to mention her in my will."

The door creaked open, and the butler entered, carrying a tray. He stepped slowly and deliberately across the room as if he were taking part in a military marching display and set the tray down on a small table between us.

He stood over the refreshments, his hands sheathed in his spotless white gloves. "Shall I pour, m'lady?" he asked.

"No need, Barrowman, thank you." Lady Dulvington smiled at Emily. "We have a catering expert with us."

"Very good, m'lady. Will that be all?"

"Thank you, Barrowman." She dismissed him, and he stood to attention, then turned and walked slowly away.

"Miss Philpot, would you?" Lady Dulvington gestured at the china teapot in front of us, accompanied by four small teacups adorned with gold rims. A matching milk jug and sugar bowl completed the ensemble. The last item on the tray was a small, crystal, stemmed glass containing a dark-red liquid.

"Of course," said Emily. She whispered to me, "Do I put the milk in first, or the tea? I'm not sure of the etiquette."

"I will take mine black, the same as Sergeant Wainwright," said Lady Dulvington, "and you may pour the rest as you please."

Emily blushed and fixed her eyes on the task in front of her. I gave a slight smile as I realised not only was Lady Dulvington's mind fully intact, but so was her hearing. Lady Dulvington ignored her tea, instead plucking the little glass from the tray and sipping from it.

"Port wine," she explained. "My one vice. The doctor told me two or three glasses per day won't harm."

"Lady Dulvington," said Oscar, as if he were beginning a formal speech. "When you rang me and requested we meet, you mentioned a private matter of some concern which you'd like my help with."

"Indeed," replied Lady Dulvington. "A most distressing occurrence, or set of occurrences."

"I'm very sorry to hear that. And this is why I asked Ms Jones and Miss Philpot to accompany me, as we, err, have been able to provide assistance to the police in a number of matters this year. Three heads are better than one."

Emily squirmed in her seat and appeared to be about to say something. I raised one finger to my lips, hoping she'd seen my gesture and Lady Dulvington hadn't.

"The police could do with assistance," said Lady Dulvington. "When I rang them to report the disturbances, they were most dismissive. I could tell that the constable I spoke with was a young, inexperienced man, unaccustomed to dealing with well-mannered people. I believe he considered me to be an old fool."

"Goodness," I said. "You're anything but that."

"Thank you, my dear. I may be in the autumn of my years, but that doesn't mean I'm stupid." She turned to Oscar. "So, Sergeant Wainwright, are you and your associates able to take my case?"

"Case? We're hardly private investigators, but I'm sure we can offer some advice," said Oscar.

Emily squirmed again.

Oscar continued. "Would you mind expanding on the matter at hand? You mentioned you believed you were being haunted?"

"I must warn you," blurted Emily, "I'm terrified of ghosts. Although, the occult fascinates me, and I'm convinced there's life beyond the grave."

"Oh, Miss Philpot," said Lady Dulvington. "I'm so glad you're here. If I knew there were unbelievers in the room, I wouldn't be so confident about asking for your help."

I turned to Oscar and gave him a half smile. He cleared his throat.

"Whatever is causing these disturbances," he said, "we may be able to help get to the bottom of them."

"Is that a 'yes', Sergeant Wainwright? Do bear in mind I plan to reward your efforts with a substantial charity donation, as per our agreement when you recovered my painting."

Oscar glanced at me and Emily. Emily was smiling at Lady Dulvington. Now she'd explained her fear, and Lady Dulvington had accepted it, she seemed much more relaxed and comfortable in our surroundings. I had the feeling Lady Dulvington wouldn't accept a refusal from us. Plus, I wanted to view the ruined house and see if this was nothing but mischievous teenagers, so I nodded at Oscar.

"It's a 'yes'," said Oscar. "We're happy to help discover the cause of these occurrences."

"What a relief," said Lady Dulvington. "I thought no one would take me seriously. That will be all for today. I must have my afternoon rest. Might we regroup tomorrow at three? I'll explain my predicament further, and I'll show you the ruins of my ancestral home, the location of the disturbing activity." She rang the hand bell again and stood. I noticed she'd finished the glass of port, but her tea remained untouched.

"Is three tomorrow acceptable to everyone?" asked Oscar. We stood as well, and indicated it was.

The butler opened the door. "Yes, m'lady?" he said.

"Please show Sergeant Wainwright, Ms Jones and Miss Philpot out, Barrowman. And note in my diary that they'll return tomorrow at three."

"Will that be all, m'lady?"

"Yes, Barrowman. You may take the evening off. Jennings will prepare my supper."

"Very good, m'lady."

Oscar took Lady Dulvington's hand. I again noticed the gesture where she didn't shake hands, just allowed people to hold hers briefly. Oscar bowed slightly, and I wondered whether I should curtsy. Emily smiled at Lady Dulvington, and she smiled back.

At some point, I knew I'd become accustomed to living on the water, but I hadn't yet. When I awoke at 9:30 the following morning, the first sound to reach my ears was the slop—slop—slop of waves on the outside of the hull and, in my bleary confusion, I imagined my barge had become untied from the dock and was drifting out into the English Channel. I threw on my dressing gown, dashed up to the wheelhouse and stared out of the windows. The sight which met my eyes was the usual view of the harbour, with the yachts, trawlers and family cruisers swaying back and forth in a stiff breeze. A uniform blanket of slate-grey cloud hovered over Redcliff, and I briefly considered returning to bed and setting the alarm for much later. Like tomorrow.

Then I remembered my plans for the day. I'd go for a long, bracing stroll along the beach, then return for a snack before heading out to Alnchurch Park with Oscar and Emily. At some point, I'd have to tackle the task I was putting off, which was to clear out the spare bedroom and find a home for everything I'd stuffed in there. It was a good thing I didn't need paid employment; I'd never have had time for anything resembling work. But the first thing on the agenda, after showering, applying makeup and choosing clothes suitable for visiting former debutantes, was to buy a double shot skinny latte from the Wicked Whelk. Now that I couldn't pop downstairs to grab one and take it back up with me, this activity required more planning and mental preparation.

The Wicked Whelk contained its usual collection of thick-jumpered fishing folk, and today they were, as every day, discussing the weather. Although the fleet sailed in almost any conditions, I'd learnt since living here that there was a fine line between it being too calm for the fish to bite and too rough for the fish to bite. There was also probably a middle point where it was too middly for the fish to bite, but the fishers didn't seem to talk about that so much. Condensation fogged the windows as it did every day, and I found Emily with a pile of empty plates in her hand in deep discussion with a man who I didn't know.

Emily's face lit up as I entered. "Morning, Shiraz. This is Sean. Sean, meet my friend, Shiraz."

"Hello, Sean. What brings you to Redcliff? Are you on holiday?"

Sean was a short man with a plump, almost boyish face, although his body seemed athletic. He wore an anorak with multiple pockets, and an unfamiliar instrument hung around his neck.

"Entities," he said. "Allow me to introduce myself. Sean Plumtree. Paranormal investigator."

"Seriously?" I asked. "Excuse me." I turned to Emily. "A word, please?"

CHAPTER SIX

"Sean, grab a seat," said Emily. "I'll bring your order." She walked in front of me towards the counter at the rear of the café. "What's wrong, Shiraz?"

"Could you please make me a double shot skinny latte," I asked, "and while the machine's making all its bubbling noises, tell me where this paranormal investigator came from. Because I smell a rat. We've been asked out of the blue to investigate a haunting, something which has never happened to us, then he turns up. To quote Oscar: 'I don't like coincidences.'"

Emily nipped behind the counter and began the coffee-making process. As the machine hissed, she wiped the nozzle of the milk frother, then leant across the counter towards me. "He strode in five minutes ago and ordered a coffee and a toasted sandwich. I assumed he was another tourist, so I made polite conversation, as I always do with our town's visitors. And he told me he was in Redcliff to investigate a reported sighting of an entity, as he called it, or a ghost. He gave me a business card. Look." She slid a small, black rectangle across the counter. In blood-red writing, it proclaimed: 'Sean Plumtree. Paranormal investigator. Explainer of the unexplained.' A mobile phone number followed.

"Did he tell you where the ghost was sighted? Perhaps Lady Dulvington called him as well as us?"

"Why would she do that?"

"Because we're not 'explainers of the unexplained' and he is? Have we just been trumped to our investigation? Is this like where the FBI arrives in a murder mystery and relieves the local detectives of the biggest case of their career?"

Emily tapped the milk jug and topped off my coffee. "You sound threatened. I didn't realise you were taking this so seriously."

"Think about it, Emily. For a variety of reasons, since I've been in Redcliff, I've become tangled in several murders, drownings and a kidnap. A kidnap of me, no less. It's almost become normal. So investigating something as benign as wails and apparitions in a ruined house is a relief. This is going to be fun. Plus, if we're successful in identifying the ghost, Lady Dulvington will reward us with a significant charity donation. It's almost like having a job."

Emily rolled her eyes. "I have a job, Shiraz. And I wouldn't describe investigating wails and apparitions as benign. You sound as enthusiastic as Oscar. Do you think we tell Sean about our case? Maybe we could join forces? He could come along this afternoon."

"Absolutely not, Emily. This is our case. Ours. Not his."

"Goodness, you are determined. Here's your coffee. If I can, I'll ask him further questions and see whether I can gather more information from him." She glanced behind my shoulder at where Sean sat reading his mobile phone. "He seems to be a very nice man, and he's so knowledgeable."

"Okay, but don't give anything away. Act surprised if he says anything about Lady Dulvington."

"Got it. Mum's the word." She poised her pen over her pad as I turned away. "Who's next, please?"

"I'm scared," said Emily, as she parked the Morris Minor outside the gatehouse. "What if, instead of us catching the ghost, the ghost catches us?"

"We're not in an episode of *Scooby Doo*," I said. "And Lady Dulvington hasn't asked us to catch any ghosts, just to discover what's making these noises."

Oscar smoothed down his Macintosh and adjusted his trilby. "I feel a fraud for taking Lady Dulvington's money. This will all turn out to be something quite normal. Teenagers trespassing, gathering in the ruins."

"Maybe," I said. "Let's knock and see what she has to say."

Oscar thumped the door three times, and we heard footsteps from inside the house. The door was immediately opened by the butler, dressed as immaculately as before.

"Good afternoon, sir," he said.

"We have another appointment with Lady Dulvington. We came yesterday."

"Very good, sir. Her ladyship has informed me she'll accompany you shortly. Please wait."

He closed the door and left us standing on the step.

"Accompany us shortly?" I whispered.

"She means to the house."

"Are we driving?" said Emily. "I have room if the butler doesn't come, but that means Oscar will have to sit in the back with Shiraz."

"I'll manage in the back," said Oscar. "Lady Dulvington will naturally sit in the front."

Emily glanced to her right. "And the track across the valley looks a little rough for my car. I don't want her to become stuck."

"Shh," said Oscar. "Here she is. Good afternoon, Lady Dulvington."

Lady Dulvington appeared clad in Wellington boots, a full-length tartan skirt and a green jacket. She carried a wooden walking stick and, as she stood in the doorway, the butler handed her a woollen hat with a bobble on top. Her three Corgis fell over each other in their enthusiasm to accompany her.

"Sergeant Wainwright," she said. "And Ms Jones and Miss Philpot. Thank you so much for coming."

"Our pleasure," said Oscar, bowing slightly, as seemed to be the custom. "Do we plan to visit the ruins? May we offer you a ride?" He held out his arm towards Emily's Morris Minor, standing in the driveway outside the gatehouse with its roof pulled back.

Emily grimaced.

"It's very kind of you to offer, Sergeant," said Lady Dulvington. "But allow me to drive my Land Rover. The track to the old house is rather dilapidated, and we must ford the river. There is a bridge, but it's only wide enough for foot traffic. I suspect the Morris, lovely as she is, may prefer not to get her shoes wet. And three muddy dogs might not be good for her upholstery."

"Thank you for thinking of my car," said Emily. "She's an old girl who prefers to take things easy."

"As am I, Miss Philpot. As am I. Forgive me asking you to wait while I fetch my vehicle."

Lady Dulvington entered an outhouse behind her home, and we heard an engine's starter motor. The noise persisted for some time, followed by the rattle of an agricultural vehicle. A khaki-green off-road car appeared around the corner with Lady Dulvington at the wheel.

"Hop in," she shouted, and we opened the three other doors and jumped into a car with muddy floors, torn, green leather seats and Corgis taking up much of the space. Emily and I squashed around them and were rewarded with panting in our ears.

"This vehicle's sixty years old," said Lady Dulvington, "and only has nineteen thousand miles on the clock. In my younger days, I used to drive her into Alnchurch and Redcliff, but I allowed my driving licence to lapse years ago. On the odd occasion when I venture into town, Jennings drives me. I rarely get behind the wheel anymore."

Lady Dulvington let out the clutch, and we lurched up a gravel drive with grass growing along a central strip. Spring was bursting out of the ground and all over every tree, and the warm May temperature gave me a lightness in the chest at the promise of summer. Lady Dulvington pointed at the hedgerows. "Isn't it wonderful to see all the birds nesting?" she said. "It makes my heart sing to be alive."

"I love nature," said Emily. "You're so lucky to have this private land."

"Thanks to my grandfather. He refused to sell large tranches of the estate to developers in the 1950s. The downside was, we couldn't afford the immense sums needed for Alnchurch Park to be restored, and the poor old house fell to pieces bit by bit. I've been approached many times by people wanting to chip away at the edges of my land to develop new housing estates, but I've refused them all. What would money bring me at my age, when I have such scenery?" She held her arm out of the open window.

In front of us, a gentle valley opened out with a river running through it. Mature trees in full spring leaf lined the banks, and huge old oak trees dotted the slopes. The view was very *Wind in the Willows*, and I smiled as I inhaled the scent of moist earth.

"This is beautiful," I said. "How far does your land extend?"

We stopped suddenly at the banks of the narrow river, and one of the Corgis plopped off my lap into the footwell. Lady Dulvington pointed her finger out of the passenger window. "To our left, the boundary is the row of poplar trees on the horizon. Behind us, the road you entered from. The windmill stands in the far corner above the old orchards. To our right, the estate comprises all the fields you can see, although those are not our cows; we lease the land for a peppercorn rent to a local farmer. And in front of us, the opposite side of the valley is all ours. This was where I grew up, and this will be where I die."

"I trust you're not going to do that yet," said Oscar.

"I'm eighty-nine, sergeant, and I plan to live to one hundred. After that, I'm in the hands of the Lord."

"Quite," said Oscar. "Or whatever happens after we pass away."

"Where is the house?" I asked. "I know it's a ruin, but I thought we'd have been able to glimpse it in the distance?"

Lady Dulvington turned her head to me in the back seat. "D'you see the copse of trees halfway up the slope, beyond the river?"

"Yes."

"My ancestral home is in the middle of those. Grandfather planted many of the trees as a windbreak, and I'm afraid they've rather taken over. Shall we carry on?"

The Land Rover lurched down a slope, and Emily and I gripped a Corgi each. The dog in the footwell swayed around and attempted to climb back up onto the seat with us. We splashed into the shallow waterway. Plants grew in the water, and I stared out of the window at a large trout who swam against the current, matching its speed so he remained in one spot, his body waving languidly back and forward.

"Look," I said. "A fish."

"That's Tommy Trout," said Lady Dulvington. "He's probably twenty years old. I'm glad to see he's still alive. I like to think he's a descendant of the fish I used to watch here as a young girl."

"It's idyllic," said Emily. "It makes me want to paint it."

"Doesn't it?" said Lady Dulvington. "Once this matter is concluded, you may visit to set up your easel."

"Oh, um, I don't actually paint," said Emily. "It's just something I've often thought I'd like to do."

"Then you should follow your desires. Life's too short for might-have-beens."

We continued up the opposite side of the valley away from the water, then Lady Dulvington steered left onto a narrower track which headed into the woods. As the trees closed around us, Emily grabbed my arm. "This is where it gets spooky," she said, glancing up at the canopies obscuring the light.

"It's just a wood," I said, squeezing her hand.

"That's what they said in *The Hobbit*. And *Harry Potter*."

"Those are stories, Emily. This is real life. We're fine."

A branch cracked as the Land Rover drove over it, and Emily gripped my arm harder. The trees thinned, and we parked next to a jumble of stone walls. Most were at waist height, some at head height, and two stood to the level of a single storey. We could see the rough layout of rooms, with gaps where doors and windows had been, but nature had grown over much of the house, and it was obvious it could never be restored to its former splendour.

Lady Dulvington stepped out of the car, jammed her walking stick into the ground at an angle and surveyed the ruin. We opened our doors to allow the Corgis to tumble out and joined her.

She turned to us, sighed, and said one word.

"Home."

Lady Dulvington stepped over a long stone lying on its side, mostly buried under moss. "Here we are at the back door," she said. "The exit to the garages, where Grandfather kept the car. Then here in the north wing was the main dining room, where Grandfather would carve the roast every Sunday. We'd sit around the oak table and watch him slice the meat. He never permitted the staff to do that; it was his ritual as head of the house."

"You speak about your grandfather a lot," I said. "It sounds as though you were very fond of him."

She sighed. "He adored me, and I him. After my father passed away, he left everything to me."

We walked across the outline of the dining room and through a gap where a door must have once been.

"This was the grand hall," explained Lady Dulvington, as a Corgi lifted its leg against the remains of a fireplace. "It's the oldest part of the house, dating back to the 1500s. In my day, an enormous chandelier hung from the ceiling in front of the grand staircase to the rear. Staff would greet guests arriving for a function here, after which they would show them to their rooms upstairs."

I looked upwards and tried to imagine what the space had been like when Lady Dulverton was a little girl. Behind where the staircase must have been, the walls appeared older and thicker. They were also the most complete surviving walls, reaching several feet taller than me. I closed my eyes and imagined the voices of lords and ladies entering the main door behind me and seeing the grand staircase before them.

Lady Dulvington led us through a gap on the opposite side of the main hall. Her dogs scattered and sniffed around the ruins. "This," she said, "was the main reception room, where my grandfather received our guests. At Christmas each year, the gardeners would cut a tall pine tree from the estate, and they would erect it in the corner. Then the staff decorated it. I must confess, I was a little precocious in my childhood, and I took it upon myself to instruct them exactly where to hang each bauble."

We laughed, and I glanced at Emily to see her reaction, as Lady Dulvington relived events of over eighty years ago.

Oscar stopped and gazed upwards at where a grand ceiling once had been. "Lady Dulvington," he said. "You mentioned your father predeceased your grandfather. Why?"

Always the detective, Oscar.

Lady Dulvington perched on a low wall and rested her stick between her knees. The Corgis joined her and settled near her feet. She sighed. "My father spent all his life in poor health. He suffered from one of those illnesses which modern medicine can cure, but in those days before antibiotics were widely available, it had to be managed as well as it could be. My grandmother took care of his needs. Then she passed away and, at the age of fifty, my grandfather was left to care for a semi-invalid man in his late twenties. So he did what any man of means would do in this situation; he employed a nurse. These events were before I was born, you understand. The nurse was a girl of twenty-one who came from a family in Alnchurch village. She was assigned to care for my father day and night and to live in the big house with my grandfather, my father and several other staff. Human nature being what it is, she and my father began a clandestine relationship. But my grandfather discovered their dalliance, and he sacked her."

"Gosh," I said. "How harsh for the poor girl."

"That was how things were in the 1930s. But the story doesn't end there. Grandfather replaced the nurse with an older woman, which to his mind would prevent a repeat occurrence. Then, months later, the young nurse returned. She knocked on the main door, the one the servants would never be allowed to call at, and she announced to the butler that she was pregnant."

"Pregnant by your father?" I asked.

"That's right. Grandfather was beside himself and couldn't fathom what to do. The village girl demanded to marry my father and live at Alnchurch Park as if she were born to the aristocracy, which would've been scandalous. Then my grandfather, together with his butler and housekeeper, hatched a plan. My grandfather agreed to allow the girl to live at the house in secret until her time came. Then, she was immediately to hand the child to the housekeeper, who would raise it here.

The explanation they planned was that the housekeeper's sister had died in childbirth, and the baby had come to Alnchurch. Following the birth, my grandfather would give the nurse a sufficiently large sum of money to persuade her to leave, to guard her secret and forget the matter."

"What an incredible scheme," I said.

"Oh, you'd be surprised how many similar plans were made by all classes of people in the days when society viewed illegitimacy as a crime. The plan would've run perfectly, were it not for one factor my grandfather failed to consider." Lady Dulvington paused, and her eyes became distant. "The primal wound."

"What's the primal wound?" asked Emily.

"The separation of a mother from her child. As soon as the child was born, the nurse fell in love with her and refused to give her up. But my grandfather insisted on sticking to the original plan, although he permitted the former nurse to live here for a few weeks after the birth. When the baby was finally taken from her, she descended into deep melancholy and..."

Lady Dulvington paused, and her eyes moistened.

"...and she hung herself, right here from the staircase bannisters in the grand hall."

CHAPTER SEVEN

I gasped and covered my mouth. Emily shivered.

"That's a fascinating story," said Oscar. "Forgive my next question, please, Lady Dulvington, but how have you come to know all these details?"

"My grandfather told me." She set her jaw and met his eyes. "The child was me, Sergeant Wainwright. And that's why I was so close to my grandfather. He loved me as if I were his own. The daughter he never had."

"Do you think your birth mother is the ghost?" asked Emily.

I clenched my teeth and glared sideways at her. The pain of being pregnant and never seeing your child was something which stayed with you all your life. I knew the primal wound all too well from my youth, although every day I buried in my soul the eternal emotions of my own unplanned pregnancy.

"Ah, the ghost," said Lady Dulvington. "How clever of you to make the connection, Miss Philpot. But I'm afraid I can't provide you with an answer. I don't know why this restless spirit has chosen now to make an appearance, and I can't identify it. That's why you're here."

Emily shivered, glanced around and grabbed my arm.

Oscar sat heavily on a wall and puffed loudly. I could tell his patience was being tested, but he was far too respectful of Lady Dulvington to accuse her of making things up.

"Lady Dulvington," he said. "You rang me because you believed you were being haunted. The local police offered no assistance, which is hardly surprising, as supernatural occurrences aren't a police matter. I agreed to help you, but I'm sure we'll find this is nothing more than mischievous teenagers playing some kind of a prank. How many times have these events occurred, and who else, apart from you, has heard these noises and witnessed the figure in white?"

"Sergeant Wainwright, you've confirmed my decision to employ you. I never forgot your dogged determination to recover my painting, and I know you'll apply the same diligence until we discover the reason for the visitation. I've heard the wails on several evenings, as has Barrowman. Jennings, my daily, has also mentioned hearing howling. And we've all caught sight of the distant figure in white floating through the trees."

"Have any of you ventured up here after dark to investigate?"

"I'm an old lady, Sergeant. Barrowman's no spring chicken, either. Today's trip is my first back to the house in a long time. I'll need to rest and recover before Jennings arrives to read with me. And I couldn't ask her to come up here alone in the dark. If this really is young people up to no good, as you suspect, who knows what might happen?"

"Lady Dulvington, may I be frank?" said Oscar. "I have no experience with the supernatural. I have, though, over thirty-five years of investigating mysteries and solving crimes. If you wish, together with Shiraz and Emily, I can scrutinise this matter as I would a crime. I propose to interview people, gather evidence, make case notes and narrow down suspects until we know the identity of the person who is disturbing you, whether they be someone living, or, less likely, someone departed. That is the extent of my, or our, expertise. We don't have any fancy ghost-detecting equipment, nor do we have any means to deal with the so-called ghost once we identify it."

"And that," said Lady Dulvington, "is why I have brought other people onto the team."

"The team?" said Oscar.

"The team," repeated Lady Dulvington. "You, with your experience of running investigations, will be the head. As you've implied, I hope you and Ms Jones and Miss Philpot will perform the bulk of the investigation, interviewing people and gathering evidence. Though I believe many of the interviewees may have to be spoken to through a medium."

"I know a medium," I said.

"You are welcome to co-opt others as needed. However, as you admit, you lack supernatural experience. I have therefore retained the services of one Sean Plumtree, a ghost hunter of some repute. I responded to his advertisement in the magazine *Country Lady*, and he's introducing himself to me here tomorrow. I expect you three to work closely with him and leverage off each other's experience."

"We've already met him," said Emily. "He called into my café, and he seems very knowledgeable and pleasant."

"Good. I'm glad to hear he's settling in. I've accommodated him at The Harbour Guest House. And in response to your final point about what we do with the ghost, I shall consult a priest, who may be able to advise what action to take with this restless soul."

"There's no need to involve a vicar," said Oscar. "They won't be able to help with teenagers playing pranks."

"That's for you to find out, Sergeant. As per our arrangement when you recovered my stolen painting, there will be a significant donation to a charity of your choice. Do you have one in mind, or would you like me to donate it to the Police benevolent charity again?"

"I don't feel right accepting funds like some kind of paid private investigator, but if you insist, Shiraz and Emily are current members of Redcliff Marine Rescue, and I, of course, run the gift shop for that organisation."

"That's settled," said Lady Dulvington. "I'll deposit ten thousand pounds with them as soon as we conclude our business."

"Ten thousand pounds," I whispered to Emily. "Murph will be pleased. That'll go halfway towards buying the new FLIR."

"Mr Plumtree is, of course, being recompensed under a more commercial arrangement," said Lady Dulvington. "Let us return to the gatehouse now."

"Will we be able to talk to your butler and daily help?" asked Oscar. "We should start with eyewitnesses."

"I'm seeing Mr Plumtree tomorrow, and I expect you'll need to meet him first, discuss tactics and make a plan of attack before you interview anyone. I'll call you to confirm the time he's coming."

"The ghost hunter?" Oscar puffed and rolled his eyes. "Why not? The more the merrier."

"I can't believe I agreed to this," said Oscar, as we sat in the living room of my barge, which now appeared to be transforming into spook HQ.

He sipped from a glass of refreshing, cold, clear Chardonnay, an appropriate drink for a warm, early summer evening. "If it wasn't for the generous donation," he said, "I'd politely decline. Here's how I think we should approach the matter. We'll visit the ruins by night, lie in wait for the teenagers or whoever's perpetuating this nonsense, photograph their antics and provide the evidence to Lady Dulvington. Case closed, as Emily might say."

"We can't do that," said Emily.

"Why not?"

"Because Lady Dulvington's investing ten thousand pounds in this exercise, plus whatever she's paying the ghost-hunter chap. If we solve the case in one evening, she'll feel ripped off. We have to justify our existence. And there's no way I'm sitting in a ruined mansion at midnight waiting for a ghost to pop out. Even if they are a teenager dressed in a sheet."

"Emily's right," I said. "We need to go through the process. We don't want to insult her, do we, Oscar?"

Oscar sighed. "This really isn't me. I'm not used to working on a fee for services basis. All I can offer is to proceed as if this were a crime."

"We should begin an investigation sheet, like we have in the past," said Emily. "But instead of the deceased in the centre, we could have a circle for the ghost."

"Great idea," I said. "And we could have circles for every suspect we believe could be the ghost. Supernatural ones on the left and human ones on the right."

"The paper will have a distinct list to starboard, then," said Oscar. "There won't be too many names on the supernatural side."

"We have one already," said Emily. "Lady Dulvington's birth mother. To my mind, she's the most likely. She died a violent, unnatural death in the building where Lady Dulvington and her staff have seen the ghost. I'm so tempted to say, 'Case Closed' right now."

"But why did she wait over eighty years to haunt the place? I know nothing about the habits of ghosts, but I can only imagine they'd materialise shortly after death."

"That's not always the case," said Oscar. "North of here is the location of the Battle of Sedgemoor, fought in the 1600s.

Even after four hundred years, people say they still see the apparitions of soldiers marching across the fields."

"I thought you didn't believe in ghosts."

"I said 'people say.' They may not be reliable witnesses."

We laughed.

"Here's what we'll do," I said. "Oscar can be in charge of investigating the theory that the ghost is actually a human playing tricks, and Emily and I can study the supernatural side. We'll recap regularly to discuss our findings and exchange notes."

"I'm very happy with that arrangement," said Oscar. "I can't investigate something which doesn't exist."

The sound of AC/DCs 'Thunderstruck' blared from his pocket. He answered his mobile phone. "Hello, Oscar Wainwright speaking. Good evening, Lady Dulvington. Certainly, you have been busy. Yes, between the three of us, we can attend. Very good. See you tomorrow. Goodbye."

"That was Lady Dulvington. Our investigation's beginning. She's calling a team meeting tomorrow afternoon together with the ghost hunter, Sean Plumtree. He's showing Lady Dulvington some equipment and explaining what he needs from her. Directly after that, we can all interview the butler, Barrowman. And then, in the late afternoon, her daily help, Jennings, will call in to read with her. We can speak with her too."

"Don't forget, Shiraz, we must be back here by six," said Emily. "We have marine rescue academic training in search patterns."

"I've remembered," I said, frowning at her. "So we won't be able to stake out the ruins tonight?"

"I'm not convinced I'm visiting them any night."

"I intend to look at them further by day," said Oscar. "You both could come with me. But enough nonsense about the supernatural. What I'll be looking for is discarded beer cans, cigarette ends, vapes and so on. Evidence of teenagers partying up there."

"I'm happy to investigate by day," said Emily. "Oh. We need a name."

"A name?" replied Oscar. "What d'you mean?"

"Teams of people investigating things always have names. Like the *Famous Five*, or the *Secret Seven*."

"How about the *Gullible Gang*?" he said. "Because there are no such things as ghosts."

CHAPTER EIGHT

"Sergeant Wainwright," said Lady Dulvington, rising from her chair as the butler showed us into her living room. "How good of you to come again."

The Corgis jumped up and turned in circles at the sudden intrusion of six more hands available to deliver pats and tummy rubs.

"And I see Ms Jones and Miss Philpot have accompanied you once more. May I introduce Sean Plumtree, from Plumtree Paranormal Investigations. I hope you will all become well acquainted, as I expect you to cooperate closely to solve this business."

Sean stood and held out one hand. "Emily, lovely to see you again. And your friend, Shiraz."

Emily blushed, took his hand and glanced at me.

Sean appeared completely different without the hood of his anorak. His Tommy Hilfiger shirt and Diesel Jeans showed a man of taste, far from the nerdy person I'd taken him to be.

I smiled at him. "Sean, this is retired Sergeant Oscar Wainwright, who Lady Dulvington originally approached."

Oscar shook his hand but avoided eye contact and gave him a tight smile.

"I'm so pleased we'll be working together," said Sean to Oscar. "Lady Dulvington outlined your background, and I think your investigative knowledge, together with my technical skills, will help us understand her paranormal encounter."

"Mr Plumtree tried to explain his equipment to me," said Lady Dulvington, "but I'm afraid I'm a fossil with electrical and mechanical objects, and it's all gone over my head."

"I'm sure I'll have the same problem," said Oscar, "but Shiraz and Emily might understand. What's the agenda today, Lady Dulvington?"

"Before we get into that, who'd like tea? Jennings brought a home-made cake this morning. She really is a wonder, that girl."

We all indicated we would. Lady Dulvington rang the little bell, and the butler opened the door.

"Barrowman," she said. "Tea for five, and please cut five slices of Jennings' Victoria sponge."

"Very good, m'lady." He reversed out of the room.

"The purpose of our meeting here today," said Lady Dulvington, "is to agree on a plan of action. The four of you must concur on the approach needed, and I hope you can agree where your respective responsibilities lie."

"We've already begun that task," said Oscar. "Shiraz and Emily will study whether there is any historical aspect. You mentioned to us your father's nurse, for instance."

"I don't object to you referring to her as my mother," said Lady Dulvington. "Even though I never knew her, she was more of a mother to me than anyone else."

"Your mother, then. Emily has begun a list, and her name is at the top. The only name, to be honest. Meanwhile, I will investigate whether there is a human element."

"A human element?" asked Lady Dulvington. "Do you really imagine a living person could be responsible for the wails we've heard? What about the sightings of the figure in white?"

"We'll investigate all angles, Lady Dulvington. We won't rule out anything."

"If I might butt in," said Sean, "I've had many years of experience investigating supernatural entities, and I gather this is your first?"

"It might be," said Oscar, sitting back and folding his arms. "What d'you have to add, Mr Plumtree?"

"In matters of this type, where the manifestation is as described, it's very rare for the noises and apparitions to be explainable as someone playing a prank. I can only think of one case, which, to be quite honest, I was hesitant to accept, where the sightings could've been attributed to anything physical. In the matter of Alnchurch Park, I'm convinced we will find this to be a genuine, supernatural haunting."

"Of course you'd say that," said Oscar. "Because if it isn't, there's no reason for you to be here."

"Gentlemen, please," said Lady Dulvington. "I would like you to co-operate with each other, not argue about your respective abilities. I have employed you, Sergeant Wainwright, because of your investigative track record and your persistence not to let any loose ends lie until you've arrived at a result. And you, Mr Plumtree, are here because you have experience in explaining the unexplainable."

"As it says on my card," said Sean, pushing his shoulders back and giving Oscar a triumphant look.

"Has Mr Plumtree seen the ruins?" I asked, in a bid to bring the conversation back on track.

"Yes," said Sean. "Lady Dulvington took me up there this morning. I ran my EMF scanner over the site to see if I could detect anything unusual, but the readings stayed below normal levels."

"What's an EMF scanner?" I asked.

"Electromagnetic Field Scanner. Electromagnetic fields are present in the conscious mind, and they don't go away, even when you die. The existence of electromagnetic fields is a very good sign supernatural entities may be present."

Oscar puffed. "You can buy those scanners from any electrical hardware shop."

Sean blinked rapidly and appeared to be about to retort.

"What other equipment d'you have, Sean?" asked Emily. "I am fascinated, although I admit I'm a little scared."

"As you should be. The human mind is trained to accept things the way they're supposed to be. If we pass a man walking down a street, we take no notice, even if we have never seen that particular man before. But if we pass a man walking down a street and we observe his feet are floating six inches above the pavement, and then we notice he has scaly claws instead of hands, our reaction is fear, because that's not how things are supposed to be."

"I think if I saw a man hovering above the pavement with claws for hands, I'd run a mile," I said. "But you were going to tell us about your equipment?"

"Yes. Besides my EMF scanner, which is a small device and not completely infallible, I have two tripod-mounted digital cameras with units attached to them, designed to detect and capture images in the light spectrum which the naked eye cannot see."

"Ooh," said Emily, "Would that include ghosts?"

"I prefer to use the word 'entities', Emily. Often, we can't tell what these devices have picked up until we review the footage on a computer later. And lastly, I have an ultraviolet light. Entities live in a bluer world than we do, and they see everything in ultraviolet. My light attracts them, much in the same way a butterfly is enticed to visit certain kinds of flowers."

Emily folded her hands in her lap and leant towards Sean. I could've sworn her eyelids fluttered.

"And where is all this equipment?" said Oscar. "D'you have it with you?"

"I've only brought my EMF scanner today." He pointed to a bag resembling a camera case resting at his feet. "I'll bring everything else when we visit Alnchurch Park at night."

"Visit the ruins by night?" squeaked Emily.

"Of course," said Sean. "How else will we detect an entity which only makes itself known after dark?"

Oscar hmphed to himself.

"It's good to have you on the team," I said to Sean. "As you've correctly observed, we three have no supernatural experience. But we have been involved in clearing up several mysteries, and I'm glad we'll be putting our heads together."

"Excellent," said Lady Dulvington. "I'm so pleased with your cooperation." The door creaked open. "Ah, here's the tea," she said. "Together with Jennings' wonderful cake. She really is a treasure. I'm so looking forward to reading with her later."

Barrowman laid a tray on a low table between us, much to the interest of three long, snuffly noses. Emily poured five cups of black tea, and I smelt the wonderful aroma of Earl Grey, the perfect afternoon refreshment. I made a mental note to try to always attend the gatehouse in the afternoons; the chances of Lady Dulvington being able to provide my vital morning double shot skinny latte were minimal. Although it was rapidly looking like many of our visits would be after dark, and I wasn't sure how Emily would react.

"Lady Dulvington," I began, after we'd each selected a slice of Victoria sponge, which was, as reported, so light and fluffy it weighed no more than a handful of makeup removing pads. "Might I suggest we begin our investigation by naming who might be a suspect? And by the word 'suspect', I don't wish to intimate they've done anything wrong. Simply the suspected identity of the restless soul. We have your birth mother for a start. Can you help us with names of anyone else who lived here?"

Lady Dulvington sighed and fed morsels of cake to the three Corgis. "Where to begin, and how far back to go?"

"If I might make a suggestion?" said Sean. "May we use the word 'candidate' instead of suspect? And begin by listing anyone who died on site, as it were, particularly anyone who met a violent end. In my not-inconsiderable experience, very few souls stuck on earth are people who've passed away in hospital from influenza."

"In that case," said Lady Dulvington, "I can think of three. My birth mother, who we have already listed, is the first. The second…"

"Just a minute," said Emily. "I usually have the role of scribe in our investigations. Let me make a couple of notes on my phone."

"I've watched Jennings use her computer," said Lady Dulvington. "She seems to manage quite complicated tasks on it. I still use pen and paper." She laughed, and Oscar joined in.

"The second person who passed away at Alnchurch Park," continued Lady Dulvington, "was a workman in the early 1950s. The poor chap fell off the stable roof and died instantly."

"D'you remember his name?" asked Emily, her finger poised over her screen.

"Davies. Freddy Davies. He was only twenty. I was in some distress over his death, as I was seventeen, and I confess I found him somewhat alluring."

I smiled with what I hoped was an expression of commiseration. "And the other person?"

"Several staff died in hospital following the World War II bombings, and I'm ashamed to say I didn't know all their names. But the only one who died on site was my adoptive mother, the housekeeper, Mrs Hutchings. I felt no emotion about her death, which may sound strange, but only someone who wasn't brought up by their birth mother would understand."

"How old were you when she died?" I asked.

"Eight. My father's illness claimed his life before the war and, after Mrs Hutchings died, I pretty much brought myself up. Naturally, people believed I was rather an unruly tearaway, but I was always close with my grandfather. He was my only family, after all. Anyway, apart from those three, I'm unaware of anyone else who died violently at the estate." She glanced around, and her gaze settled on Sean Plumtree. "And I can't help with any events in previous centuries. There may be hundreds of people who died violent deaths here between the 1500s and the 1900s, and I'm completely oblivious."

I rubbed my chin. "I wonder if the parish church would have records?"

"Possibly," said Oscar. "Although the further back you dig, the vaguer the records become. I tried to trace my family tree when I first retired for a hobby. Once I'd gone beyond my great-great-grandparents, the task became tricky. In some parish records, even people's names weren't recorded properly, let alone their reason for death. I spent ages trying to track down a lady called Sarah Eastham who would've been my great-great-grandmother. I had little success, then I realised I already had all her details, but under the name Sarah Miles. The same person had been recorded with two completely different names in two places."

"I'll ask Sister Florrie for access to the records," I said. "That may unearth more candidates."

"Meanwhile," said Oscar, "we'll visit the ruins during the day. I'll put my detective's hat on and see if I can find any earthly clues. That's the best value I can add."

"I'm itching to visit by night and set up my equipment," said Sean. "That's when we'll get the best results."

"Before we do any of that," I said, "we need to interview the two people who've witnessed these apparitions. Barrowman the butler and Miss Jennings. Would Barrowman be free to talk now?"

"Of course," said Lady Dulvington. She rang the handbell, and the door opened immediately, as if the man had his ear to the keyhole.

"Yes, m'lady?"

"Barrowman, would you mind joining us? We'd like to ask you some questions."

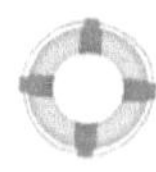

CHAPTER NINE

"Questions, m'lady?" asked the butler.

"About the noises you heard, and the white apparition."

"Very good, m'lady." He remained standing.

"Do sit, Barrowman," said Lady Dulvington, as if she were addressing one of the Corgis.

"Of course, m'lady." He perched uncomfortably on the end of the Chesterfield sofa.

"Mr Barrowman," I said. "Could you tell us about the noises you heard coming from the other side of the valley?"

He cleared his throat. "I was polishing the silver in the kitchen after dinner a few nights ago. Her ladyship had retired, and Miss Jennings had departed after her habitual evening reading session. Night had fallen, and I had drawn the curtains. It was then I heard a wailing sound. My first thought was that it was an animal; perhaps a hare or fox directly outside the window, or stags fighting in the woods. But it continued and intensified in volume like no animal noise I'd heard before. I paused in my labours and opened the window to peer out into the darkness. As soon as I did that, it stopped."

"Did you hear it again?" I asked.

"Yes. The following evening. Miss Jennings had again recently left, and I was setting out the breakfast cutlery for the following morning when I heard the same noise. I opened the front door and stepped outside. That night, there was a moon and, as I gazed across the valley towards the ruins, I saw what I imagined to be a distant figure dressed in white, drifting through the trees. Then the noise ceased, the figure vanished, and I returned inside."

"Did you tell anyone?"

"I considered whether the entire thing had been my imagination. Or maybe the noise really was animals, and the figure in white a large owl. Then, the following evening, Miss Jennings approached me. She said she'd heard a horrible wail when she was cycling away from here towards her home in Alnchurch, and she asked me if I'd heard or seen anything. Naturally, I told her I thought the noise to be animals, and the apparition to be a barn owl, but her young ears are better than mine, and she became convinced that I'd seen a spirit. The following day, she told Lady Dulvington, and that, I presume, is why we're having this conversation."

The effort of pushing out so many words seemed to have exhausted him, and he stood, nodded at us, then addressed Lady Dulvington. "May I clear the tea, m'lady?" he asked.

"Thank you, Barrowman. We'll let you know if we need to speak to you again."

"Very good, m'lady," he said. He picked up the tray and left.

"What did you make of that?" I asked everyone, once the butler had closed the door.

"The butler's a sensible man," said Oscar. "He believes the noises are most probably animals, and the apparition in white is nothing more than a barn owl. I've heard they're often mistaken for ghosts, as they swoop silently through the night."

"I disagree," said Sean. "A classic case of an anomalous phenomenon. The wailing, the appearance of a phantom; it wouldn't surprise me if I discovered evidence of materialisation when I investigate further."

"What's materialisation?" asked Emily.

"Materialisation is a physical manifestation of a supernatural substance. Sceptics have derided it as being created by clever trickery, but there have been enough sightings by respected, credible witnesses to lend credence to its existence."

"Utter rubbish," I heard Oscar mutter under his breath.

Lady Dulvington addressed Sean Plumtree. "It is, of course, your job to explain the unexplainable."

Oscar shifted in his chair and crossed his legs.

She stroked a spare Corgi and looked up at him. "Which is why I have brought this team together; the diverse minds and approaches will solve the mystery."

"Is there anyone else we could speak to?" asked Oscar. "We've interviewed Barrowman. Later on, we'll be speaking to your daily help. Could we perhaps meet the gardener? Stokes, was it? And anyone else who has visited the premises in the last week."

"Apart from me and my three staff, the only person who ever visits is my son, Lucas. He's supposed to come once a week for afternoon tea, but he rarely turns up. If you talk to him, please be sensitive when mentioning anything about ghosts. He had a terrible experience when he was a boy. He was cycling home from scouts in Redcliff, down the steep hill from the windmill. When he reached the flat section at the bottom, he said he heard footsteps. Scrunch-scrunch-scrunch, he told me, the noise going around and around in the road. It was dusk, but he could still see in the twilight. And he said the footsteps kept circling but there was no one there. He ran home, and when he entered the house, he was trembling, saying he'd heard a ghost. Ever since then, he's had a morbid fear of the unknown. So tell him, by all means, but make sure he understands about the noises and sightings, and say they're coming from the ruins."

"Was he here when you heard the noises?" I asked.

"No. His visits are brief affairs. He's a troubled soul and struggles to find the time for his elderly mother."

"How unkind," said Emily. "We should all spend as much time as possible with our parents before it's too late."

Oscar cleared his throat. "Would we be able to speak to Stokes, then?"

"Of course. He'll be here at seven tomorrow morning, and he'll depart by three. But I know tomorrow he has a big day planned, clearing a fallen tree. Would Thursday morning be acceptable?"

"Thursday it is," said Oscar. "And your son?"

"Sunday would be the only convenient time for him, if he actually comes. And we may have the entire matter cleared up by then."

"We may, but in case we haven't, could I ask you to contact him and reserve time for us on Sunday afternoon?"

"I can, but what, exactly, are you wanting to ask him? I can't see how he could be connected. He hasn't heard the noises, and he hasn't, to my knowledge, visited the site of Alnchurch Park for a very long time. He wouldn't go within a mile of it, if he thought it was haunted."

"Leave that to me," said Oscar. "No stone unturned, remember? That's why you've asked me to help."

"How right you are, Sergeant. I should leave the investigating to you. Now, if you'll excuse me, I'd like to freshen up before Jennings gets here."

"What time does she arrive?" I asked.

"Four-thirty. We read together for an hour or so, then she leaves, and I take a light supper before bedtime." She rose, and we all did the same. I watched her sweep out of the room in a cloud of perfume and Corgis and hoped I was as athletic in my late eighties.

"We need our investigation sheet," said Emily, once Lady Dulvington had left the room. "We have more suspects than any of the murder cases we've investigated, and I'm losing track."

"Murder cases?" asked Sean. "Investigated? How very Agatha Christie."

"It's not important," I said. "Just a game we play. Emily, let's list the names we have on your phone, together with anything we know about them. Then we'll transcribe the notes to an investigation sheet tomorrow. I'll buy one of those gigantic pieces of card from the newsagent."

"Okay. Let's start with our, shall we call it, earthly list."

"That should be our only list," said Oscar.

"I'm glad Lady Dulvington isn't present to hear your comment," said Sean. "She seems to be a very spiritual lady."

"Then let's hope we can convince her otherwise. I'm sorry, Mr Plumtree. I don't subscribe to your hogwash, and I see your activities merely as a way to take advantage of gullible, elderly people."

"Oscar, Sean," I thumped the arm of my chair. "Are we going to work together to solve this, or fight amongst ourselves? Lady Dulvington's counting on us to figure out the mystery. We'll begin by listing everyone, no matter how unlikely, and we'll rule people out as we go."

Oscar grinned. "The student has become the master. First suspect, Lady Dulvington."

"Why would you include her?" asked Sean. "She's the one who's asked us to investigate, so she won't be the suspect, as you call them. I think we should put Lady Dulvington's deceased birth mother at the top."

"May I repeat Shiraz's words?" replied Oscar. "We'll begin by listing everyone, no matter how unlikely. I appreciate you haven't been through this exercise before, but we do get results with it. Write down Lady Dulvington, Emily."

Emily typed on her phone.

"Next, the staff," I said. "Barrowman the butler, Jennings, the daily help and Stokes the gardener."

Emily giggled. "Just like playing *Happy Families*."

"I remember that game," I said. "Mr Bun the baker and so on. And lastly, we should include the son, Lucas."

"This is ridiculous," said Sean. "He doesn't live here, he's terrified of ghosts since an apparitional experience as a child, and I can't think of a single reason he would assume the persona of an entity."

"Dear me," said Oscar, "we are using some fancy words, aren't we, Mr Plumtree? 'Entity' and 'Persona'. Anyone would think ghost hunting's a recognised profession."

"Are you always so condescending?" asked Sean. "Ghost hunting is, for your information, a recognised profession. I have a degree in parapsychology from the University of the Paranormal in California, USA. Majoring in anomalistics."

Oscar smirked. "An eminent institution, I'm sure. I could probably apply for my own qualification from there by paying fifty dollars."

"Enough," I said. "Will I need to split you two up? Now we've written down the human suspects, let's write down the, err, inhuman ones?"

"The correct terminology is 'paranormal'," said Sean. "The word 'inhuman' would be insulting to ghosts. I propose that, as part of my role as the only"—he glared at Oscar—"person here with paranormal experience or qualifications, I define the correct naming convention for the supernatural world. We must stop referring to your list as 'suspects' and instead call them the preferred term of 'candidates'. I'm fine with the use of the word 'human' for people who are alive, and for people who've passed on, we should employ the word 'entity'. Ghost, phantom, ghoul, demon and so on became unfashionable, even controversial, some years ago."

"Now I've seen everything," said Oscar. "A woke ghost hunter."

"Paranormal investigator, please," said Sean.

"I do hope Lady Dulvington can't hear you two arguing like schoolboys," I said. "She's powdering her nose, or whatever she calls it, on the other side of that door."

"Let's begin listing the candidates," said Emily. "First, Lady Dulvington's mother. Does she have a name?"

"Call her 'DBM' for now," I said. "'Dulvington Birth Mother.'"

"Then the workman who fell off the ladder, Freddy Davies, I already noted and also the adoptive mother. DAM. Dulvington Adoptive Mother."

"You've forgotten one," said Sean.

"And who would that be?" said Oscar. "The Phantom of the Opera? Dracula? Frankenstein?"

"None of those three you've mentioned are technically entities," said Sean. "The Phantom of the Opera was discovered to be a..."

"Yes, yes, yes, I get it. You have the"—Oscar made air quotes with his fingers—"parapsychology qualification. Who have we forgotten, then?"

"The phenomenon heard by Lady Dulvington's son. The footsteps circling in the lane."

"That happened decades ago, and hasn't been heard by anyone since," said Oscar. "Don't even bother to write that down, Emily."

"No stone unturned, Sergeant?" said Sean.

Oscar hmphed and folded his arms again.

"Here's what I think we should do," I said. "We'll continue to interview the human candidates, as you call them, Sean. Then we'll arrange one night to all go up to the ruins. Sean can set up his equipment, and we'll lie in wait to see if the ghost appears."

"You can all lie in wait," said Emily. "I'll lie in bed. There is no way you'll drag me up to a ruined mansion after dark. Anyway, I have a café to open at 6:00 a.m., so I can't stay out all night, regardless of the reason."

"Would you come up with me during the day, Emily?" asked Sean. "I could set up my equipment tomorrow afternoon and ensure it's working as I need it to be. Then I'll leave the tripods and stands there, and we'll return one night to wait for any entities to make an appearance. Perhaps you'd like to help me set up?"

"Oh," said Emily. She blushed and fiddled with her phone. "We'll see. I may have to visit the wholesaler tomorrow."

"Before you help Mr Plumtree with his spook catching contraptions," said Oscar, "we should regroup on the barge to create the investigation sheet. Could you send the notes from your phone to Shiraz? And while you're at the café tomorrow, we'll transcribe them onto the sheet. Once you're available, we three will perform our usual analysis, making notes about each suspect..."

"Candidate," said Sean.

"...each candidate and giving them a score. The same as we have before."

We heard a bell clang from the hall and the sound of the butler's footsteps, followed by the front door creaking open. Muted voices conversed, then the door to the living room opened, and Barrowman stood to one side of it.

"Mesdames and Messieurs," he announced, "may I present Miss Jennings?"

A young lady walked in and glanced around the room. "Oh," she said, taking a step backwards. "I didn't realise Lady Dulvington had guests. I'll wait in the dining room."

Her tweed skirt, roll-necked, orange jumper, brown utilitarian shoes and thick-rimmed glasses gave her a very serious look, and her red hair was pulled up in a bun, which wasn't the fashion I associated with people in their twenties. A green-and-gold brooch clashed with her top, and I withheld the temptation to offer fashion advice.

I stood and held out my hand. "Miss Jennings, do come in. We were talking about you."

"Me?" She pulled her head back. "What's this about?"

"Nothing to concern yourself with. Lady Dulvington has asked us to speak with you. Please, sit down. My name's Shiraz; may I introduce Emily, Oscar, and finally Sean."

Miss Jennings perched on the edge of a high-backed chair and gripped her phone. She pressed buttons on it as if she were messaging someone, which I found rather rude.

"What's your first name?" I asked. "I can't call you Miss Jennings for ever."

"Zoe," she said. "But my university friends call me Zozo."

"Oh, you're at university?" I asked, in a bid to get her to focus on me and not her phone. "What are you studying?"

"Engineering, specialising in mechatronics. I travel to Bristol twice a week, then the rest of the classes are online." She raised her eyes. "But what d'you want to talk to me about? I'm only here to read with Lady Dulvington before her supper."

"We'd like to ask you about the noises you heard coming from the opposite side of the valley," said Oscar. "The wailing, or whatever it was."

Zoe Jennings gave a theatrical shudder. "I never want to hear it again. That howl sent a chill down my spine. Like nothing I've heard before." She returned to her screen.

"Mr Barrowman believed it to be some kind of animal," said Oscar.

"I've lived in Alnchurch all my life, and I've never heard an animal make that noise. I know the sounds hares and foxes make; they can get pretty noisy in spring. Badgers too, although they grunt more. The deer roar, and that can be very alarming. But, this. This was something from beyond the grave."

"I'm interested that you use that expression," said Sean. "I'm also very interested in your engineering background, as a unit in my parapsychology degree was in psionics; applying the principles of engineering to the study of the paranormal."

"That sounds odd," said Zoe. "It's not a module in my course."

"So you're convinced this wasn't an animal?" I asked her.

"Definitely not. It was an unearthly noise." Zoe continued to talk to us while tapping on her phone. "If you asked me to describe the howl, I'd say it sounded something like…"

HAWWWWWWWWWOOOOOOOOOOOOOOOOOOO

We jumped, and I felt a cold shiver down my spine as a horrendous bawling began in the distance.

CHAPTER TEN

"There it is," said Zoe. She jumped up and raced to the window. "See? An inhuman noise."

The noise stopped, then the connecting door to the bedroom opened, and Lady Dulvington marched in with her three dogs trotting at her heels.

"Did you hear it?" she asked, jabbing her finger at the window. "I nearly fell off the bathroom stool. This, Sergeant Wainwright, is what's haunting me."

The Corgis competed for her attention, and she patted them in turn.

"Our friend's early tonight," said Oscar, staring out into the gloom. "It's not even dark yet. Nightfall's still several hours away. The so-called entity has decided to make an early appearance."

"I vote we walk up to the ruins and search for the phenomenon," said Sean.

"No way. I'll stay here," said Emily. "You won't catch me walking up there at all, now we know the noises come during the day as well. In fact, Shiraz, could we go home? It's all a bit too spooky for me, and we have marine rescue training in an hour."

I stared out of the window, but I couldn't stretch my neck far enough to see the opposite side of the valley.

"We've all heard it now," said Lady Dulvington. "So nobody should be in any doubt. Ms Jones, have you finished speaking with Miss Jennings? Because it's 5:00 p.m. and time for an hour spent with a book before supper."

"We have, thank you. And we've had a discussion about our next steps. We'll return on Thursday morning to chat with Mr Stokes, as arranged."

"Thank you so much for coming." The little bell tinkled in her hand, and the butler opened the door. "Barrowman, please see our guests out."

"Very good, m'lady."

We stood in the driveway to the gatehouse, staring across the valley. All we could see was the trees surrounding the ruins halfway up the opposite slope. Although it was still several hours until sunset, the woods lay in the shadow of the surrounding slopes.

"I've a good mind to set up my equipment tonight," said Sean.

"What?" said Emily. "You're going to sit up among the ruins all night, waiting for the ghost to emerge? I'm still shaking from that horrible sound."

Sean nodded. "It wouldn't be the first time. I'll return to my accommodation to check all the kit's ready, anyway."

"We have marine rescue training now," I said to Oscar and Emily, "which should finish by 7:30. Why don't we grab a takeaway afterwards and return to my barge to eat it? We can have a chat and try to work out what's really going on."

"An excellent idea," said Oscar. "Much more productive than sitting waiting for a teenager in a sheet to jump out from behind a bush."

Murph addressed his laptop primarily by yelling and shaking his fist, which didn't seem to improve its performance.

"Clodhopping catamarans. You'd think these things would become easier as technology moved on, but I swear they're getting harder and harder."

Emily and I sat with the two other recruits going through basic training, Colin and Paul. They'd joined Redcliff Marine Rescue after us and hadn't completed so many on-water duties. I wondered if either of them could help Murph in his current predicament.

Murph's gaze floated between the laptop and the screen behind him. He repeatedly pressed buttons on the TV remote, wiggled the mouse across his desk and stabbed at the keyboard, all to no avail.

"Have you tried turning it off and turning it on again?" asked Colin.

"The TV or the laptop?" asked Murph.

"Maybe try both."

We waited while the TV screen turned black, then the manufacturer's logo appeared, followed by an image with the Redcliff Marine Rescue logo and the words 'Search training' underneath it.

"I remember having to do that on the computers at school back in the 1980s," said Murph. "I can't believe we still have to switch them off and on to get them to work. Anyway, thank you, Colin. Welcome, everybody, to marine rescue training tonight. This evening, we'll be studying search patterns of several types by day and by night. I know you've all had practice on the boat, some of you even in a real search situation, but I'd like to increase your knowledge to a level where I can sign you off as proficient. Once you've completed tonight's academic training, there's a written assessment, then a practical on the boat when I'll ask you to regurgitate your learning and demonstrate any search skills I choose to assess you on. Is everyone okay with that?"

We all nodded in agreement.

Murph clicked the mouse, and I noticed the expression of relief on his face when a new slide appeared on the screen.

"First," he said. "The two searches we use most often. Can anyone tell me their names?"

"Expanding square and parallel track," said Emily.

"Correct. In what circumstances would we use each one? Someone else? Shiraz?"

"We'd use expanding square when we know where the person entered the water," I said.

"Correct. And parallel?"

"Parallel is where you're searching a larger area of ocean, back and forward, and have much less idea where someone or something is."

"Yes. Well remembered. Okay, expanding square. As mentioned by Shiraz, we use this where we know someone, or something's last position. We start at that point and work our way outwards. Does anyone remember how we do it? Who'd like to draw it out on the whiteboard?"

"I will," said Paul. "We did it last week on the boat." He stood, walked to the front and picked up a black marker. "We go in a straight line away from the first point, then turn ninety degrees to the right…"

"Whistling winches," said Murph. "To starboard, Paul, not to the right."

"Sorry, Murph. To starboard. We travel the same amount of time on this leg as we did on the first, then we turn ninety degrees to starboard again and travel for double the time. Then again, and so on and so on."

His pattern on the whiteboard resembled a snail drawn by Picasso, an ever-expanding whorl of square lines.

"That's perfect," said Murph. He clicked to the next slide on his presentation, and the screen showed a neater version of Paul's drawing.

"Could anyone tell me how we know when to turn to starboard?" asked Murph. "There are two correct answers. Colin, d'you know?"

"We could plot the search pattern on the instrument screen. That's what we did last week."

"That's the newer way. What would you do if your instruments were broken?"

"Would someone time the legs and call out to the skipper when to turn?" I asked. "I remember doing that on one of my first shifts."

"Correct," said Murph. "And the final question on expanding square searches: what's their biggest disadvantage?"

I shrugged. Emily shook her head. Paul and Colin remained silent.

"That's okay if no one knows," said Murph. "It's the whole point of training, to fill the gaps in our knowledge. The biggest problem with expanding square searches is that we never cover the same place twice. So if we start here,"—he jabbed his finger at the centre of Paul's diagram—"then we head away from the spot to the first turning point and make the ninety-degree turn to starboard, if we pass the person in the water without noticing them for any reason, we'll never see that spot again. And that's a massive problem. It's very easy to miss a human head in the water. If they're not wearing a bright-yellow lifejacket, or even if they are, they're nearly invisible."

His hand poised over the mouse. "Here's an advanced question, as I'm sure none of you will have done this training yet. There's another type of search we can do which doesn't cover as much water as the expanding square, but it does reduce the chance of missing someone. Note I said 'reduce', not 'eliminate'. Can anyone think of what I'm talking about, even if they don't know what it's called?"

"Could we somehow go back to where we started?" I asked. "So if we'd completed four legs of the expanding square, maybe we could about-turn and retrace our steps back to the beginning."

"Ye-es, you're on the right lines," said Murph. "Yes, to going back to the start point. But not retracing our steps. There's a more efficient way." He took a board eraser and wiped across Paul's drawing with big sweeps, then picked up the marker.

"We start again from the same central point. But we plot a pattern which looks like this."

He drew a circle around the starting point and segmented it into six so it resembled a spoked wheel, like the counters in a Trivial Pursuit game. Then he wiped off the outer edges of alternate segments, and the drawing became three triangles, with their points meeting at the central starting point.

"This," said Murph, tapping the board, "is a sector search. In real life, we'd take the boat to the starting point; the place where whatever we're looking for was last seen, or where we estimated the casualty had drifted to. We'd drop a buoy or a fender in the water to mark the spot. Then we'd head off down the side of one of these triangles until we reached the outer edge of the circle. We'd turn 120 degrees along the edge of the circle, then when we reach this point"—he tapped the board again—"we'd turn 120 degrees again so we're now heading down the other side of the triangle back towards the centre. The rescue boat would pass the buoy we'd dropped, and then head out along the triangle on the opposite side. We'd repeat this, constantly passing back through the most likely place where the casualty would be. My diagram shows a simple sector search, but there are more advanced ones with concentric patterns of triangles. But for the purpose of our training, this is the one you need to know."

"I like this one," I said, "because if there's a strong current, or tide, the person in the water will move at a similar rate and in a similar direction to the buoy we dropped."

"Correct, Shiraz," said Murph. "I'm impressed."

"Show off," whispered Emily, smiling at me.

"Right. Line searches. There are several types of these."

Murph's presentation continued with more diagrams with searches useful for combing close to beaches, searches used in river estuaries and searches where multiple boats were taking part. The diagram resembled a freshly ploughed field.

Then Murph marched to the side of the room, clicked a switch, and we were plunged into darkness.

CHAPTER ELEVEN

I blinked and glanced around the black room.

"Night searches," said Murph's voice from near the light switch.

"This is scary," said Emily. "I can't stop thinking about ghosts." She gripped my arm.

Murph continued in the dark. "We're on the boat, in pitch black. What's the biggest challenge compared to day searches?"

"You can't see so far," said a voice which I thought was Paul's.

"Exactly," said Murph. He switched the lights back on, and Emily's grip on my arm loosened. "You can't see so far, or at all. To be honest, it's rare for a night search to have a good outcome. If we're called out on a search in the late afternoon or evening, whoever's out there needing our help better pray we find them before dark. Our hopes of success once the sun's gone down are greatly reduced. However, we have tools to improve our chances. Who can list them?"

"Torches," said Paul.

"Correct. We carry three LED torches on board. They're much brighter than the old bulbs we used to have. What else?"

"Spotlights on the boat," said Colin.

"Yes. We have six roof-mounted spotlights and two hand held ones. Between all of those and the torches, we can light up a decent chunk of sea. But it's still nowhere near as bright as daylight, and we can't see nearly as far. What else do we have to help us?"

"Radar," said Emily.

"Radar helps us avoid colliding with things at night and makes us more visible to other craft. When we're searching, it's really only useful if we're looking for a boat. Humans don't show up on radar. But we carry something they do show up on. Shiraz?"

"FLIR. Which stands for Forward Looking Infra Red."

"Well remembered. The FLIR detects body heat. With it, we can find a person in the water if they're alive. How many FLIRs do we carry?"

"Two," said Emily. "One hand held and one on the roof."

"Yes. Except the one on the roof's starting to let us down. We need to replace it sooner rather than later. Okay, that concludes tonight's training. I'll see you on the boat on your next duty, and we'll put all that into practice."

"There's a simple explanation for all of this," said Oscar.

He sat at one of the stools in my barge that evening, leaning on the galley counter. I stood on the opposite side and Emily rested her arms on the end.

"We know there are no such things as ghosts, and…"

"Lady Dulvington believes there are," said Emily. "As do I."

"I'm on the fence as to whether they exist or not," I added. "As I mentioned, I knew a woman in London who was a medium, and she made a lot of money from movie stars and other famous people who needed to consult her."

"There you have it," said Oscar. "Proof if ever there was. She made money out of it, so she was hardly going to admit ghosts didn't exist and cut off her income stream, was she?"

"All right, Oscar, let's say you're right, and there are no ghosts, what else could Lady Dulvington have seen or heard?"

"Voices coming from the ruins could simply be trespassing teenagers. And the figure in white could be someone wearing a white dress. Or a barn owl, like Barrowman believes."

"You seem very convinced."

"I am. And when we visit tomorrow, you'll believe me."

"What did you think about that butler?" asked Emily. "He was pretty scary. He reminded me of Herman Munster. But without the comedy."

"Lady Dulvington said he'd been with the family all his life," I said. "But the other staff are comparatively recent."

"So he'd remember Alnchurch Park when it was in its heyday? Before the war."

"He couldn't have. How old d'you reckon he was? Seventy, maybe eighty? The war ended in 1945. But she would. Lady Dulvington would've been a young girl during the war. That would have been terrifying, living in a big house like that with bombs dropping through the roof."

"Ooh," said Emily. "The entity must be someone killed there in the war."

Oscar thumped the counter. "Entity? You've been spending too much time with Sean Plumtree. For the umpteeth time, Emily, there are no such things as ghosts. We will, I am convinced, find a rational explanation." He glanced at the brass, nautical clock above my fridge. "Right. I need to give Cadbury his evening walk. Shall we meet at two-thirty tomorrow?"

"Come to the Wicked Whelk," said Emily. "I'll lock up and we'll drive over there."

"Good idea. I'll prepare for our second visit to find this mysterious phantom. *The Phantom of Alnchurch*, by Andrew Lloyd-Webber. I can see it running for years. Goodnight, ladies." He laughed, rammed his hat on his head and hopped off the stool.

"Goodnight, Oscar," I said. "See you tomorrow."

He nipped up the steps through the wheelhouse, and I heard the door close.

"I wish Oscar wouldn't ridicule me," said Emily. "He can be very stubborn. Of course ghosts exist. There have been too many sightings all around the world to explain everything away as mischievous teenagers."

"I'll keep an open mind," I said. "Although, tomorrow morning, I might do a little research of my own."

"Now you're being mysterious. What research?"

"Sister Florrie left her hat behind at the bargewarming. I'll stroll up to the vicarage to return it and ask her what her beliefs are about the paranormal."

The last time I'd walked up the path towards the clifftop, I was chasing a young lady who subsequently came to a tragic end. I made a mental note to restart my exercise regime as I didn't remember being this puffed then. Today, I had my Christian Louboutin sneakers on too, which should've made things easier, not harder. I paused halfway up, sipped my takeaway coffee, turned and stared at my barge in the harbour below.

My barge. Mine. As the first home I'd ever owned all by myself, I was determined to stamp my mark on her. Perhaps I'd paint the outside a different colour to the brown and beige she was now. I couldn't really change the internal layout, but I could fluff it up a bit. Maybe I'd buy an interior design magazine from the newsagent. From my current viewpoint, she looked longer than she felt when I was on board. I reckoned, at eighty feet, she was probably the longest vessel in the harbour. Bigger than any of the trawlers. I tore my eyes away from her and carried on up the path, pushing brambles aside as I strode.

The wind at the clifftop buffeted me, and I stared at the open sea below, where angry whitecaps rode towards Redcliff. They broke over the harbour wall in giant clumps of white mist, soaking any souls walking on the opposite side. I smiled and silently congratulated myself on my acquisition. My home.

Redcliff Manor lay to my right and West Cove to my left. I strode past the point where I'd tried to talk a Ukrainian girl out of jumping and marched on along the cliff path. Ghost hunting, I thought to myself, was infinitely less stressful than murder suspect hunting.

Not least because ghosts didn't exist. Said Oscar.

Or maybe they did, as Sean believed, and Emily as well.

The tower of All Saints Redcliff appeared in the distance, and I bent my head into the gale.

DING DONG DING DONG

"Hello, Shiraz, what a wonderful and unexpected surprise." Sister Florrie threw her arms around me and squeezed the air out of my lungs. "Marie, Marie, she called. Is there any tea in the pot? Make a fresh one for our guest." She held my hand and dragged me into a large kitchen, where laundry hung from a wooden contraption hoisted above a solid dining table.

Sister Marie stood with her back to us at a white butler's sink. She lifted one rubber glove-covered hand to wave.

"Please, sit," said Sister Florrie. "Anywhere you can find a spot."

I pulled out a chair at the rectangular wooden table. Sister Florrie occupied a similar chair at the head of the table, one with arms.

"I brought your hat back," I said, pulling the beret from the inside pocket of my coat.

"I wondered where I'd left that," she said. "Did I forget it after your housewarming?"

"You did. And thank you so much for coming to bless my barge."

"My pleasure. The Lord will keep her safe."

Sister Marie laid two cups of tea in front of us, and Sister Florrie dropped three cubes of sugar into hers.

"It's very kind of you to walk up here in this gale just to return my hat," said Sister Florrie. "It's not the type of weather I'd like to be out in for a stroll along the clifftops. But then, I'm built more solidly than you, and I'm less likely to blow away."

I laughed. "Actually, there was something I wanted to ask you about. A rather sensitive subject. I'm not sure how to express it, as it's a strange request."

"Try me," said Sister Florrie. "I've had plenty of strange requests in my time."

"Okay. This would be one of the strangest. A local resident believes she's being haunted, and I wondered if you had any records I could study which might detail people who've suffered violent deaths."

Sister Florrie folded her hands in her lap and sat back. "That is an unusual request. Not the kind of thing we're asked for every day. Baptisms, yes. Weddings, naturally. Funerals, they're a part of life. But hauntings? Not too often. Although, I am the correct person in the town to consult about performing an exorcism."

"Goodness. Have you ever performed an exorcism?"

"Once, at a former parish where residents of an old building known as The Coach House reported a poltergeist. The spirit was slamming doors night and day, which was keeping them awake."

"What did you do about it? This is fascinating. I thought you'd dismiss my story as a load of old codswallop."

"Quite the opposite. We take the matter of restless souls very seriously. Sister Marie and I painted crosses on both sides of every door. Then we walked around the house chanting appropriate prayers and sprinkling holy water."

"Gosh. Did it work?"

"The people living in The Coach House didn't complain again, so I'd say it did. The poor soul's at rest in the good hands of the Lord now."

"Where would you start investigating a ghost? I have an image of people setting up all kinds of complicated equipment, then waiting silently for nights on end until something goes bump in the night. Which may well be what happens with this one."

"I'm sure that's what it's like in the movies, but in the Church of England, the process is considerably less dramatic. The first step would be to find out why the spirit is restless.

What's keeping them from passing happily up to heaven? Why are they stuck here with us mortal beings?"

"And how would you do that? It's not as if you can ask them. Or can you? Do you have some way of communicating with the dead, like a medium I knew in London?"

"Nothing so direct. Sometimes, I wish I did. No, as you requested, we'd start by poring through the parish records to work out who the soul might be. Is there any record of someone dying at the location where the restless soul's been reported, for instance?"

"Was that the case with the exorcism you performed on the poltergeist?"

"Yes. We searched back through the records and discovered a young man had died in The Coach House in the 1800s. The cause of death was given as 'convulsions', some kind of fits, I suppose."

"Is the cause of death always given in parish records?"

"That depends completely on the vicar at the time. At Redcliff, sadly, my predecessors seem not to have been the most detailed of men. And they were all men; Sister Marie and I are the first female incumbents. But in Alnchurch, in the late 1700s, a Reverend Albert Eden began a painstaking work of recording the cause of death of everyone he buried, sometimes in great detail. And his successors appear to have kept up the tradition."

"Of course, the local resident I'm referring to lives in Alnchurch Parish, not Redcliff. I should probably ask the vicar there. Sorry, I may have wasted your time."

"Not at all. You're in luck. Several years ago, there was a flood at Alnchurch vicarage, and much of the church paperwork was relocated here for safekeeping during the clean-up operation. The parish records were never returned. You could look at them now."

"Goodness. That is lucky. But I presume they're on paper? It's not like we can enter search terms into a computer."

"Unfortunately, you're right. You're going to have to be the computer."

"How many records are there?"

"That depends how far into the past you want to look. They go back to the 1600s, although prior to Reverend Albert Eden's time, they merely stated the person's name and date of death. Let me show them to you."

Sister Florrie led me into her study. She opened a double-doored, full-height cupboard behind her, glanced up and down, then waved her arm at three stacks of leatherbound books, each over an inch thick. She tugged one from the top of a pile and crashed it onto her study desk.

"They look heavy," I said. "Are they arranged chronologically?"

Sister Florrie laughed. "They're probably not arranged at all. Let's open this one." She flipped the A3-sized volume open somewhere near the centre, and the pages rustled.

I ran my eyes across the entries. In cursive writing, neatly scribed with a black fountain pen, were lines of names. Each entry recalled a person who'd meant something to someone once. Fathers, mothers, brothers, sisters. I read one random entry. Silas Bowflower, died 3rd January 1804, aged 32, following a fall from a horse.

"There must be hundreds in each book. We'll take ages. How many volumes are there?"

Sister Florrie pointed her finger at the cupboard and totted up the books. "Eleven. I'm afraid this will be a labour of love. We'd better get started."

DRING DRING

An old-fashioned Bakelite telephone rang at her elbow.

"Excuse me," said Sister Florrie. She picked up the handset, and I heard one side of her conversation. "Hello, John. Yes, very well, thank you. No, no, I quite understand. You must've been shaken by that experience." She paused and glanced at me. "That's very interesting and may tie in with someone I'm meeting with now. I'd be delighted to help. Bye, John. God bless."

Sister Florrie replaced the handset and sat back in her chair, which creaked. "May I ask who the local resident is who reported this matter to you?" she said. "It's not Lady Dulvington, is it?"

CHAPTER TWELVE

I furrowed my brow at Sister Florrie's question.

"It is Lady Dulvington who asked us to investigate. How did you know?"

"Because she's approached my colleague, John Woodman, to ask if he has experience with restless souls. He's the vicar at Alnchurch, so properly he's the correct person for her to consult. But he had a nasty experience on the road outside Alnchurch Park; Lady Dulvington's home. He fell off his moped late at night on his way back from our house, and he'd prefer not to attempt the steep hill again. So he's asked if Sister Marie and I would take care of it. And given our previous success, I've agreed. Shall we start on the records and see if we can gain insight into which soul needs a helping hand up to Heaven?"

"This is such a fascinating place," I said, as we picked our way through the ruins that afternoon. "I'm standing here, trying to imagine what it must've been like living in a house of this size, with staff and gardeners, chauffeurs and maids."

"Isn't that how you lived in London?" said Emily.

"Not exactly. We had a cook and a cleaner at home, neither of whom lived on site, plus a chap who tidied the garden and did maintenance. To be quite honest, Monty and I were out at functions much of the time, so none of them had that much to do. The house didn't get very dirty, and the only meal we really ate there was breakfast. And often that was a coffee from the local café. Here at Alnchurch Park, I can imagine it was something like *Downton Abbey* on a smaller scale."

"I would agree," said Oscar. "I wasn't born when the house was destroyed in the war, of course. I've seen photos at Redcliff Historical Society, and I remember they show a double-fronted, three-storey building with a carriage drive." He swivelled his head left and right. "Lady Dulvington said where we're standing was the main entrance hall, with rooms to each side for entertaining and eating. And the grand staircase rose behind us, in front of the thick, tall walls."

"I'd love to have seen that when it was complete," I said.

"We will be home before dark, won't we?" asked Emily. "I don't really want to hear that wail again during the day, let alone the night."

"You're standing where it was coming from."

"Don't say that, Shiraz, or I'll leave now."

"What would you like to achieve today, Oscar?" I asked. "What should we be looking for?"

"Any sign of recent human activity, however small. I'm still convinced these disturbances are caused by local teenagers playing pranks, so I'd suggest trying to find the kind of evidence they'd leave. Beer cans, bottles, takeaway food wrappers, cigarette ends and so on. Maybe if we start at the far corner and search a room each?"

"I'm not doing it by myself," said Emily. "What if that wailing starts?"

"You and I can search the bigger rooms between us," I said. "Oscar, you take the smaller ones."

"Good idea. And remember, don't only look at the ground. Check to see if anything's stuck in the gaps between the stones."

Emily and I stumbled over rocks and the remains of low walls until we reached the front right corner of the house. Moss-covered blocks lay piled at odd angles, as if a giant child had suffered a tantrum over a box of Lego.

"Where do we start?" I asked. "This is a massive task."

"One room at a time," said Oscar. "Look for anything artificial and new."

"Like this?" said Emily, bending down and picking up a crisp packet.

"Exactly," said Oscar.

"But that could've simply blown here," I said. "That doesn't prove teenagers were holding midnight parties."

"We'll gather everything we find and examine it all at the end. Don't discount anything."

We'd brought a dustbin liner each, and we all wore disposable gloves. In the first room, I found the ring pull top off a can, a rusty screw, a sweet wrapper and a short length of electrical wire. Emily added several cigarette ends to her crisp packet and some funny-shaped pieces of plastic. I glanced to my left and watched Oscar crouching down, peering into gaps in the walls.

"It's all just litter," said Emily. "Lady Dulvington's fooled us. She's made up a story about a ghost so she can get us to pick up her trash."

"I'm sure she could employ someone to collect trash for less than she's donating to Marine Rescue. And what about the mysterious wailing sound?"

"Don't remind me. Oh. What's this?"

Emily plucked a shiny metal rod from between two rocks. It was four inches long, around one quarter of an inch in diameter and had tiny holes drilled through it at both ends. She showed it to me.

"It could be anything," I said. "Maybe it's part of something the gardener uses, a mower perhaps. Keep it, and we'll inspect it more closely later."

We continued to pick through the rooms. None of Oscar's hoped-for beer bottles or cans made an appearance, but we did discover several cigarette butts. We met Oscar sitting on a wall to the right-hand side of the house.

"This part," he said, "was the outbuildings, or staff quarters. I reckon it's a relatively recent addition. When I say relatively recent, I mean only two hundred years old."

"Which is the oldest part?" I asked.

"It would have to be the central bit, where we entered, which dates from the 1500s. The building grew outwards from there, and wings and outbuildings were added as the centuries passed."

"It's so sad, that the house has all been destroyed and poor Lady Dulvington's forced to live in the little gatehouse," said Emily.

"To be honest," said Oscar, "even if the building had survived, I'm not sure she would've been able to hang on to it as her home. So many of England's stately homes have been turned into hotels or conference centres to raise money for their upkeep. Those which haven't, their families are desperately trying to keep them open by running guided tours or letting them as wedding venues. Or, as with *Downton Abbey*, which you mentioned, renting them to film companies to use as sets for period dramas. The building you know as *Downton Abbey* is, in fact, called Highclere Castle. It's around a ninety-minute drive from here. Anyway, enough talking. Let's head back to Shiraz's and compare what we've found." He held up his bin liner. "Forensic clues, as I would've called them in the old days."

"Hang on," I said, as Oscar prepared to upend his black bag on my dining table. "Let me cover it with something first."

I found a plastic tablecloth in a drawer, removed a candle from its position as a centrepiece and laid the covering on the table. Oscar tipped his bin bag out, and Emily and I followed suit.

"Oh," I said. "Would it have been helpful to mark which room each item came from, rather than mixing it all up?"

"Not really," said Oscar. "What we're trying to do is prove this so-called ghost is a product of human activity. Is there anything among our collection of junk which could help? I was hoping for a haul of discarded beer cans, but maybe these particular teenagers don't drink." He fingered through the litter and spread it out on the table. "We have a salt-and-vinegar crisp packet, several Silk Cut cigarette butts, a ring pull from a can and what looks like a gold earring, of all things. Then there are several odd artefacts. The long rod with the holes drilled in each end, three nuts, none of which have bolts they screw onto and these funny-shaped items. He held up three black, plastic shapes with rounded ends.

"They look like blades from a fan," I said. "A tiny one, like a desk fan. Oh, look. Here's another one exactly the same."

"Do they mean anything?" he asked. "Or are they red herrings?"

"Could they simply be rubbish which has blown there over the years?" asked Emily. "I reckon if you did a litter pick in Redcliff Municipal Gardens, you'd assemble a similar collection of junk."

"Maybe," I said. "Although some of these things are too heavy to have blown in the wind." I held up the piece of metal. "This rod, for instance. What have we achieved from the exercise, Oscar?" I smiled. "Has it helped us rule anyone out?"

"No. And it hasn't proved the teenager theory, either. We need to begin our investigation sheet. At the moment, we have a list of suspects, or candidates, as Mr Plumtree insists on calling them, on Emily's phone. Then we have a heap of other clues such as this pile of stuff, which may not amount to anything conclusive, and we have the interviews with the butler and Miss Jennings."

"And with Lady Dulvington herself," said Emily.

"Quite. We need one of those giant pieces of card again."

"The shop'll be closed now. But let's pick one up on the way back from interviewing the gardener tomorrow. In the meantime, take a seat. I'll grab us a wine each, and I'll tell you what I discovered at Sister Florrie's."

CHAPTER THIRTEEN

"Ah, yes," said Oscar. "I'd almost forgotten your mission this morning. What did our dear vicar have to say?"

"Here's the strange thing. It's a coincidence, I suppose."

Oscar puffed. "You know what I think of coincidences."

"This one is probably genuine, and here's why. I arrived at the vicarage and mentioned to Sister Florrie that one of our local residents had reported a haunting. Also, I asked her if she had any records we could inspect to see who might've died a violent death in Alnchurch. I'd completely forgotten that Alnchurch and Redcliff were different parishes and likely to have separate records. But she told me that Alnchurch's books were stored with her, as there'd been a flood at Alnchurch vicarage. She was showing them to me when her phone rang, and here's the coincidence. The vicar of Alnchurch was calling, and he told Sister Florrie that Lady Dulvington had rung him and asked him if he had experience with restless souls."

"I have a lot of respect for Lady Dulvington," said Oscar. "But she seems to be involving a lot of people in something which may have a perfectly natural explanation. If this is supposed to be some kind of a secret, more and more people are party to it. What did the Alnchurch vicar say?"

"He told Lady Dulvington that he'd prefer not be involved, as he fell off his moped coming down the steep hill to the entrance to the Alnchurch Park, and he doesn't want to take that route again."

"I don't blame him," said Emily. "It's bad enough in a car."

"Plus, Sister Florrie has even performed exorcisms, and he hasn't. He asked Lady Dulvington if she'd object to him passing the matter to his colleagues in Redcliff. So Sister Florrie said she and Sister Marie would take care of it. Apparently, their previous exorcism was some years ago, when residents of a place called The Coach House were being bothered by a poltergeist."

"I don't remember anything about that," said Oscar.

"She said it was at a former parish. Anyway, she showed me the Alnchurch parish records, and we began looking through the lists of deaths together for anything unusual. People who'd died young or died by unnatural causes."

"I'd imagine that exercise would take ages," said Oscar. "There must be thousands of records going back centuries."

"Actually, no. Before the new hospital was built with the staff accommodation, Alnchurch was a smaller parish than Redcliff. And bear in mind, the records only went as far forward as the 1970s. They're all stored at the Headland Bay Records Office now, and the parishes don't retain a copy. I began with the records from the 1940s to the 1970s, and Sister Florrie took the earlier part of the century. My records contained the workman who fell off the ladder, and I found several people who were recorded as dying following the bombing of the house, although I'd forgotten the name of the housekeeper. We also found a man who'd been poisoned by his wife in the village, and two people who drowned in marine accidents. Plus, in my records there were several young men who'd never returned from the second world war, and in hers from the first."

"We're only looking for deaths at the estate, right?" asked Emily. "Not people who'd drowned at sea or fallen on the battlefield."

"Right, but Sister Florrie kept getting distracted. Then we went back to the 1800s. The records were kept in neat writing from a fountain pen, but some words were very hard to read. And some causes of death were difficult to tell if they were natural or unnatural, such as 'nervous prostration' or 'intemperance', both of which were terms we found."

"Intemperance is an old word for drunkenness," said Oscar. "So I suppose that could have ended in an unnatural death, if the drunken person had fallen and struck their head, for instance."

"Right. But none of them occurred at Alnchurch Park except for one; a lady employed at the old windmill. On the days when there was no wind, the windmill could somehow be turned by a horse walking around in a circle. And the lady's job was to walk with the horse. She owned it and would scrunch down the lane with it to Alnchurch Park whenever its services were required. She'd walk around and around in a circle all day with that poor old horse grinding corn."

"You found this out from the records?"

"The priest at that time made very detailed entries. Plus, we rang the current vicar of Alnchurch, and he stated her headstone was in the churchyard. Her job was listed as 'Horse walker'. Anyway, her cause of death was that she fell under the horse's hooves while the horse was circling around and around the mill, and she was trampled."

"What a horrible ending," said Emily. "Did this lady die young?"

"Exactly the opposite. She was 83."

"No wonder she fell over walking around and around in circles at 83," said Emily. "I'd probably get dizzy and fall over at 30. Okay, I'm going home to bed. I need an early night."

"Yes, and while you're running the café tomorrow morning, Oscar and I will pop up to interview Mr Stokes. How are we going to get there, Oscar, if Emily's at work?"

"I could lend you the Morris Minor," said Emily, "but she's a little temperamental. A one-woman car, really."

"It's all good," said Oscar. "I'll call my friend. He runs an unofficial taxi business for people he knows."

"Mr Stokes," said Oscar, accosting him in his tool shed behind the gatehouse. "My name is Oscar Wainwright, and this is my associate, Shiraz Jones. D'you mind if we ask you a few questions? Lady Dulvington's asked us to speak with all her staff on a rather delicate matter."

"You're not police officers, are you?" asked Stokes. "Has something else been stolen?" He tugged a cigarette packet from his pocket, extracted a Silk Cut and lit it.

"Stolen?" I said. "I'm not clear about what you're referring to."

Mr Stokes sighed. "Lady D has a habit of forgetting things and firing off wild theories. Last week, she asked me if I'd seen her Land Rover. She implied it had been stolen, and she was going to talk to the police. I reminded her she'd asked me to take it to the garage to be serviced, and I'd be collecting it later the same day." He lowered his voice and tapped the side of his head twice. "I think she may be getting a little forgetful in her old age."

"You surprise me," I said. "But we're not police. Oscar was, once. No, Lady Dulvington's reported odd goings-on in the ruins of Alnchurch Park, and she's asked us if we'd investigate. She's heard mysterious, ghostly sounds."

Stokes wiggled his palms, grinned and made an 'oooOOOOooo' sound. "A ghost. How terrifying." He smirked. "She really is going batty. First it was her jewellery, then the Land Rover and now a ghost."

"Jewellery?" asked Oscar. "What jewellery?"

"Barrowman says some of her jewellery's going missing. A pair of 24-carat earrings, then an emerald brooch and finally a diamond ring."

"And how did you come to know about this?" asked Oscar. "Did Barrowman accuse you of stealing them?"

"Of course he did," said Stokes. "But I wouldn't be surprised if he stole them himself."

"Really?" I said. "I understand he's worked for her family all his life."

"Maybe he decided to steal her jewellery to sell it for his retirement? He's pretty old."

"Hmm," said Oscar. "Lady Dulvington didn't mention anything about missing jewellery to us. She's merely asked us to investigate the noises she's heard. And the apparitions."

"So she's seeing apparitions too?" sneered Stokes? "She really has lost it. Time for her to go into a home, I think."

"Are you always so disrespectful to your employer?" I asked. "On the occasions we've spoken to her, she's always seemed completely lucid. I hope I'm as switched on when I'm her age."

"Some days she is; some days she isn't," said Stokes. "It depends whether she's remembered to take her tablets."

"Could we get back on track?" asked Oscar. "Lady Dulvington's reported hearing a wailing sound coming from the opposite side of the valley in the woods surrounding the ruins. Barrowman's heard it too, as has Jennings."

"Zoe Jennings," said Stokes. "Young Zoe Jennings, the lady's maid. Have you met her?"

"Yes, on Tuesday. Why?"

"What was your impression?"

I realised Stokes had again steered the conversation away from our intended subject, and I wondered what he was trying to hide.

"She seemed pleasant enough," I said. "Lady Dulvington's very fond of her, particularly because she comes to spend time with her in the evenings, which isn't part of her employment arrangement."

"Strange, don't you think?"

"What's strange?" I asked, thinking we were the ones who were supposed to be asking the questions, not the gardener.

"Strange that a young woman studying engineering at university spends her time with an elderly lady of her own free will. Most people in their early twenties use their spare time to enjoy themselves with friends of their own age."

Oscar frowned and pursed his lips. "What, exactly, are you implying, Mr Stokes?"

"You're the detective. You work it out."

"I'm not a detective; I'm retired. Why don't you help me understand what you're thinking?"

"Isn't it obvious? She's a gold digger, after a chunk of Lady D's estate. She was originally employed as a daily maid on kitchen and cleaning duties, three mornings per week only. Lady D took a shine to her; Zoe Jennings recognised this and wormed her way in. She realised that if she befriended the old lady, Lady D might carve her off a slice of her will. She doesn't have anyone else worth leaving it to."

"What about the son?" I asked, thinking we were getting further and further from the supernatural aspect, but still wanting to hear what Stokes had to say.

"He doesn't deserve a penny," he said. "Have you met him?"

"No. We understand he calls in on Sunday afternoons."

"She'd like him to call in on Sunday afternoons. But he crashes in whenever he pleases without notice, and only visits if he wants cash. He's a waste of space, that chap. An alcoholic, constantly in and out of rehab. Sometimes he turns up, asks her for money, she gives him some, and he leaves without even asking how she is."

"You seem remarkably well informed," said Oscar. "How are you party to what appear to be private family matters?"

"Have you ever seen the movie *Icon*, Mr Wainwright?"

"D'you mean the one by Frederick Forsyth? I've read the book. Why the reference?"

"D'you remember the storyline? About how the Russian politician left a top-secret document on his desk which was stolen, and all hell broke loose trying to find the thief? They suspected spies, other politicians in their own party, competitors for the top job. And who stole it in the end?"

"Remind me," said Oscar, fidgeting and folding his arms. "Although I can't see what any of this has to do with Lady Dulvington's matter."

"The night cleaner. He cleaned the Russian politician's office every evening without fail. He took the document off the desk, and nobody suspected him, because he was always there, each night, in plain sight. Nobody noticed him. It's like me. I stand there raking leaves or sweeping the patio, and people have the most confidential discussions around me. I hear it all."

"Could we get back to the matter of the ghost?" I asked. "Have you heard wailing or seen apparitions in white anywhere here? Particularly at, or near, the ruins of Alnchurch Park?"

"Never," said Stokes. "Lady D's imagining things. I often sit up at the old house for a morning smoke. No one else ever goes there."

Oscar wiggled his eyebrows. "Exactly as I suspected. Mr Stokes, in your considerable experience as a man who knows the grounds of the estate probably better than anyone, what, in your opinion, could have made the wailing and howling heard by Lady Dulvington and the other staff?"

"Hares, probably. They sound human at night in mating season. Like babies crying at full volume. Or foxes. But most likely hares."

I leant towards him. "I feel silly for asking, but what d'you think might resemble an apparition in white floating through the woods across the valley?"

"Remember, I'm not usually here at nighttime," said Stokes. "But on rare occasions I've returned because I've forgotten to do something like switch off an electric tool which is charging. And, once or twice, I've seen barn owls flitting through the trees. They move silently, and they're mostly white. I think that's what people are calling apparitions."

"I'm convinced that's all this is," said Oscar. "My other theory was there might be teenagers on the estate up to no good, but we searched yesterday and didn't find any evidence of them. And you mentioned no one visits the ruins."

"Do you have any other questions?" asked Stokes, "or can I get back to what I'm supposed to be doing? Blackberries will overrun the track down to the river if I don't deal with them."

"Of course," I said. "Thank you for your time."

"Mark my words," said Stokes, as he collected his tools together, "that Jennings girl's up to no good. I'd be investigating her if I were you, rather than ghouls, witches and wizards." He laughed and stomped away.

Oscar thrust his shoulders back and nodded at me. "I vote we tell Lady Dulvington hares cause the sounds, and the white apparition is actually a barn owl. Stokes thinks so, and he knows the grounds better than anyone."

"We can't do that yet," I said, as a pickup truck pulled into the drive.

"Why not?"

"Because Sean's here to set up his ghost-catching equipment. And, unless I'm mistaken, he has Emily in his front seat."

CHAPTER FOURTEEN

Emily leant out of Sean's passenger window. Business advertising had either been removed from the side of the pickup truck or painted over, but it was too indistinct to see what it had said. The vehicle had large knobbly tyres which raised it some distance off the ground.

"Hi, Emily," I said. "How come you're here? I thought you needed to go to the wholesaler?"

"Oh, hi, Shiraz, hi, Oscar. I forgot you'd be at Alnchurch Park this afternoon. The wholesaler will have to wait. Sean asked me if I'd help him set up his paranormal investigation equipment."

"You and Sean are going up to the ruins together now?"

Sean leant over from the driver's seat. "It's so kind of Emily to help me," he said. "With two of us, we'll have it set up in a jiffy."

"And," said Emily, her eyes sparkling, "Sean's going to teach me how it all works. He might even let me try to capture an image of a ghost."

"Seriously? I thought they petrified you."

Emily leant towards Sean. "I can be brave when he's with me."

"Right. Got it. Okay, you guys go ahead. Sean, when will your equipment be ready for our first, um, seance?"

"It's not called a seance, Shiraz. That's a completely different exercise. In the business, we call it a paranormal stakeout."

"I'm learning the lingo," said Emily. "If we see a ghost, sorry, an entity, and it turns out to be a real entity, that's called a PSI hit. And if we think we've seen an entity, but it's actually something natural, that's called a PSI miss."

"Goodness, you are getting into this. So when can we see if we get our first PSI hit?"

"Tonight," said Sean. "After dark. Around 9:00 p.m."

"9:00 p.m., Emily? Isn't that your regular bedtime?"

"Not tonight. I'm too excited for sleep. Although, I do hope we don't see any bats."

"No. You're scared of them too, aren't you? Okay, I won't hold you up. Would you two like to come back to my place for fish and chips between setting up the equipment and tonight's adventures?"

"I would," said Emily. "Does that fit in with your plans, Sean?"

"Definitely. We can compare notes."

Emily waved, and the truck lurched off along the track towards the river and the other side of the valley.

"Paranormal stakeout?" said Oscar. "PSI hit? PSI miss? I confidently expect we'll have a lot of PSI misses tonight. I'll come along, but only to prove what a load of claptrap this all is."

We carried our fish and chips around the harbour wall to my barge. At least, Oscar carried fish and chips. I held a large, rolled-up piece of white card and a packet of marker pens which I'd bought at the newsagent.

"You don't mind if I fetch Cadbury, do you?" asked Oscar. "The poor chap's been on his own all afternoon."

"Of course not. Let's pop the food into the oven until Sean and Emily arrive. I wonder how they've got on setting up his equipment? I'm amazed Emily wants to become so closely involved with searching for a ghost, but she seems rather taken by him."

We stepped on board, and I opened the door. The roof had been in the sun all day, and the entire metal structure had acted like an oven. I stripped off my well-used Dolce and Gabbana jumper and laid it on a chair. Oscar placed the fish and chips on the counter.

"Back in ten minutes," he said, and he left to collect his dog.

I stared again around the place I now called home. My first home of my own, at 38 years old. Despite my complete ineptitude at anything culinary, everything in the kitchen had a place, and it looked very tidy. Although, thinking about it, that might've been because I didn't own any pots or frying pans. Or, in fact, any cooking utensils at all. Emily had bought me a bargewarming present of two sets of glasses, one for Champagne and one for wine. She knew me too well. Ambitiously, Oscar had bought me a kettle and a toaster, which made the assumption I was going to make my hot drinks myself instead of buying takeaways, and actually have bread in the cupboard to toast. The bargewarming party had nearly been a complete disaster when, three hours before it was due to start, I'd realised I owned no plates and only one knife and fork, which I'd probably pinched from Emily's apartment. Thankfully, she'd found a packet of disposable cutlery and brought some cardboard plates and bowls with her. I'd have to ask if she could pick me up some real crockery when she visited the wholesaler.

I swivelled and studied my new living room. The table and four chairs stood close to the counter, and the four bar stools tucked under it so I could entertain eight people if they didn't want to be too social. When I'd bought the barge, all the furniture had come with it, thank goodness, as I had no idea how any delivery company would find me on the south side of Redcliff Harbour. I wasn't even sure if I could order Uber Eats. The lounge suite I'd inherited was showing wear, but it would have to do for now.

My greatest success had been my bedroom and my bathroom. I'd managed to fit almost half of my clothes into the wardrobe, and my most important makeup products. A handy pair of hooks now displayed my essential Bio Ionic hair dryer and my GHD hair straighteners, and the pairs of shoes I wore most often were accessible under my bed.

The biggest problem was the spare bedroom. Monty had shipped all the possessions I'd left in London to Redcliff, and I'd crammed everything I hadn't found a home for in the little cabin and shut the door. I didn't want to look in there quite yet. That was a job for a gloomy afternoon when I wasn't busy being a paranormal investigator.

Paranormal investigator? That's the correct expression, right?

Three thumps sounded on the door, and I heard Cadbury's claws scrabble on the steel deck.

"Come in," I yelled.

Oscar walked down the steep steps from the wheelhouse and dumped a shopping bag on the kitchen counter. Cadbury stood at the top of the steps, tilted his head to one side and whined.

"Come on, Cadbury," said Oscar. "You can do it. This is just like that sailing boat we were on last year."

Cadbury placed one experimental brown foot on the top step, then withdrew it. He whined again.

"I can't carry you," said Oscar.

Cadbury sat and looked at him forlornly.

Oscar reached up, clipped Cadbury's lead on to his collar and tugged gently. The dog edged forward reluctantly.

"That's it, boy," said Oscar. "Down you come."

Cadbury crouched down so his belly was on the floor. Oscar tugged the lead, and Cadbury flopped down the steps and ended up on top of him.

I covered my mouth with my hand and grinned.

The dog shook himself and looked very pleased with his achievement. Oscar pushed himself to his feet. "Goodness knows how we're going to get you up those again," he said.

I grinned. "He could sneak in and out like Boots, through the bathroom window."

"Would you like a Sauvignon Blanc?" asked Oscar, reaching into his bag. "I picked up a bottle when I fetched Cadbury. Oh. Cadbury, get out of the kitchen. That may be where the most interesting smells are, but you're standing in everyone's way."

The dog turned away from the fish and chips regretfully, rotated twice, lay in a corner and sighed.

Another, more hesitant knock came at the door.

"Hello?" said Emily's voice.

"Come on down. You don't have to ask."

Emily entered, followed by Sean.

"Could I use your bathroom?" asked Sean. "Lady Dulvington offered us tea, and it's gone straight through me."

"Of course. The ensuite's in my bedroom behind you. I haven't cleared the guest bedroom or bathroom out yet."

"I miss having you in the spare bedroom," said Emily. "The other day, I even began talking to you, imagining you were in the other room." She handed me another bottle of white wine.

I hugged her. "You know you can come and visit whenever you like. It's only a five-minute walk."

"D'you miss Boots?" asked Emily.

"I miss him lying on my bed at night like an orange feline hot water bottle. I don't miss him waking me up at five in the morning when you get up, and he demands feeding. He has been to visit me once or twice on his route to the fishing boats. Anyway, we'd better not drink both bottles or we'll definitely be seeing ghosts tonight."

"Entities, Shiraz," said Emily.

"I think Sean's perfectly capable of correcting my terminology without you doing it too."

"Before he returns," said Oscar, unscrewing one wine bottle top and finding glasses, "what d'you make of him?" Oscar lowered his voice. "He seems very informed, but until he persuades me otherwise, I believe he spouts a lot of tripe."

"Don't be so scathing," said Emily, in a tone of voice I hadn't heard her use to address Oscar before. "He's clearly very knowledgeable. I'm enjoying learning from him."

"He certainly has all the jargon," said Oscar. "But it'll take a lot to convince me it's anything but nonsense. What, exactly, have you learnt that's worth repeating?"

"More than I can recall off the top of my head," said Emily. "He told me, in a recent survey, thirty-four per cent of people said they'd had experiences which couldn't be explained by normal events. You could at least give him some professional respect. He hasn't been derogatory to us."

"Shh," I said. "Here he is."

The door from my bedroom opened. I glanced at Emily and dipped my chin, a natural reaction when you've been talking about someone, and they suddenly appear.

I pulled the food from the oven and unwrapped it, ready to divide it into four.

"Something smells good," said Sean. He pointed at the bottle Emily had handed me. "I thought we'd better not arrive empty-handed."

"Thank you. Gosh, Oscar brought a bottle too. I was just saying; we'd better not drink them both; then we will start seeing ghosts. I mean, entities."

Oscar held out his hand. "Sean, I feel we haven't got off to a good start. I'm an old dog, and it's hard to teach me new tricks. I'll try to open my mind to your field of expertise."

Sean shook his hand. "I understand. I'm quite used to dealing with sceptical people; which paranormal investigator isn't? I'm very open, though, to seeing how you three work together. You mentioned you'd done some investigating in the past?"

"Nothing serious," I said. "We're not private detectives, although quite by accident, we've been involved in some curious incidents. Anyway, now we're all on the same team helping Lady Dulvington. Grab some food and take a seat in the lounge. I'll spread this white card out on the dining room table, and we can begin an investigation sheet."

I unrolled the card, then rolled it the other way to make it as flat as possible. A kitchen stool offered the best vantage point to keep my fish and chips to my left and the card to my right, and I tore off a paper towel to wipe my fingers. Grease on the investigation sheet wouldn't have been a good look. We needed to appear as professional as possible in front of Sean.

"It won't be like our other investigations," I said. "The centre circle should have the word 'Entity'. Then the candidates will be around the outside."

I poised with the black pen, then turned to Sean. "What colour are ghosts?"

Oscar rolled his eyes. "I can't believe you asked that question."

Emily glared at him.

"Traditionally," said Sean, "entities are white, but in reality they can appear in many forms. I've never seen the floating white sheet which is portrayed in cartoons. More often, they're a semi-transparent mist, properly known as an amorphous spirit."

"I can't draw a mist. So I'll draw a black outline of a ghost, like in the game Pac-Man."

"At least we'll all know what it refers to," said Oscar.

"Your turn next," I said to him. "A circle for each human candidate. Could you read them out from your phone, please, Emily?"

Emily unlocked her phone, finished her mouthful of chips and read the list. "Lady Dulvington herself, Barrowman, the butler, Zoe Jennings, Stokes, the gardener and Lady Dulvington's son, Lucas."

I drew five circles on the left-hand side of the paper, marked them 'LD', 'B', 'ZJ', 'S' and 'L'.

"Next, the non-human ones. What was the expression you used, Sean?"

"'Paranormal' is the accepted word in the industry."

"The paranormal ones. Emily?"

"Lady Dulvington's birth mother, Freddy Davies, the man who fell off the ladder, the housekeeper and the footsteps circling in the lane heard by the son when he was a boy."

I drew four circles and labelled the first three 'DBM', 'FD,' and 'H'. "What initial should I put for the footsteps?" I asked.

"An apparition of sound, rather than a sighting, would simply be called a phenomenon, so put 'P'," said Sean.

Oscar craned his neck to see the sheet. "As per usual procedure, you may wish to put a cross like a church cross next to the, err, paranormal ones."

"Goodness," I said. "You're beginning to use the terminology."

"That does *not* mean I believe in the supernatural," said Oscar. "I'm merely trying to solve a mystery."

"Are we going to give all our candidates marks out of ten, as usual?" asked Emily.

"Yes," said Oscar, "but at the moment, we don't have enough information about any of them to apply any scores. Let's jot down some notes. Do the humans first. I can cope with them better. Start with Lady Dulvington."

"Okay," said Emily. "She's 89 years old, owns Alnchurch Park estate, which includes the ruins of the old house and must have enough income to pay three staff."

"Stop," I said, popping a quick chip into my mouth. "Let me write that down." I noted Emily's comments.

"She's also physically fit and agile for her age, although she preferred driving up to the ruins rather than walking."

"Quite understandable," said Oscar. "That track's very uneven, and one of the most common causes of death among older people is falls resulting in broken bones which never heal properly."

Emily continued. "She's not only physically agile, but she also has all her marbles. She didn't miss anything while we were speaking with her."

I paused. "The gardener had a different opinion."

"Oh?" said Emily.

"Yes," said Oscar. "He reckoned she was becoming forgetful. She forgot her Land Rover was being serviced, and she's misplaced a few pieces of jewellery. Although Mr Stokes suggested the butler might've pinched them."

"Wait a minute," I said. "When we spoke with Jennings, she was wearing a very odd brooch. It looked more suited to someone of Lady Dulvington's age, and it clashed with her outfit. D'you think she's stealing jewellery?"

CHAPTER FIFTEEN

"If Jennings was pinching Lady Dulvington's jewellery, she wouldn't wear it to visit her, would she?" said Emily.

"No, but maybe she's coercing her into giving it to her. It seems odd that Stokes said jewellery's going missing, and Jennings has a fine antique brooch."

"I'm sure there's an innocent explanation," said Emily. "Maybe her own grandmother gave it to her?"

"Possibly. I think Lady Dulvington's very lucid. So I'll add Stokes' remarks under general clues until we can corroborate them. Stokes might bear a grudge for some reason. Anything else about Lady Dulvington?"

"She's quite brusque with her butler, but thinks incredibly highly of her maid," said Emily.

"Hmm. I'll note that down, but I'm not sure what relevance it has to identifying who's the ghost."

"Is this the way you usually conduct your investigations?" asked Sean. "It seems very thorough, whatever you're investigating."

"As an ex-policeman," said Oscar, "my approach has always been to note everything down, however unlikely it seems, and begin crossing things out later. And, unless I'm mistaken, we'll come onto the more unlikely candidates shortly."

"Yes," I said. "Let's complete the human ones first. What do we know about the butler?"

"He's been with the family all his life, and he's very serious," said Emily.

"Is that it?"

"Mr Stokes doesn't have a high opinion of him, and each accuses the other of stealing Lady Dulvington's jewellery," said Oscar. "I wonder if the jewellery thefts have been reported to the police? I must make inquiries."

"Next, Zoe Jennings," I said. "A university student employed by Lady Dulvington as a maid-cum-companion."

"The word I'd use to describe her is 'bookish'," said Emily. "She said she was studying engineering, majoring in something. Electronics?"

"Mechatronics," said Sean. "I'm fairly sure that means engineering machines to perform tasks usually done by humans."

"Like car assembly plants?" I asked.

"I suppose so. I don't know much about it."

"Their relationship seems to be much closer than employer and employee," said Oscar. "Just an observation."

"Then Stokes is the last human suspect we met," I said. "He's employed by Lady Dulvington as a gardener, and he seems to also perform general maintenance tasks, such as taking her Land Rover for servicing."

"He was pretty rude about her," said Emily. "In fact, he was pretty rude about everyone. Barrowman, Jennings and Lady Dulvington's son."

"Yes, the son," said Oscar. "I can't help but think he may have a more important part to play in this than we believe."

"Really?" I said. "We haven't met him, so what gives you that impression?"

"What do we know about him? He's an alcoholic, always asking his mother for money. Stokes told us he only comes to see her when he wants funds, and he doesn't seem to care much for her otherwise. Could he have created the ghost to frighten her away from Alnchurch Park? Maybe he's hoping she'll flee the estate in terror, and he'll be able to sell it to fund his addiction?"

"But he's terrified of ghosts," said Emily, "since his experience with the circling footsteps in the lane outside."

"He says he's terrified of ghosts. Maybe that's a ruse to divert suspicion from himself? Maybe he is the ghost? We really need to interview him."

Sean stood to carry his empty fish and chip wrapper to the kitchen. "This discussion is all very well," he said, "but you're approaching the problem like you're hunting a murderer. The case in hand is discovering what entity"—he glanced at Oscar—"human or not, is presenting itself as an amorphous spirit, and making these wailing sounds. Investigating people's characteristics and their relationships to each other isn't going to solve that question, is it? What we need is paranormal evidence. We need to see the entity, hear the sounds. Until then, we're just guessing."

I waited for Oscar to make some retort about how this was all mischievous teenagers, or maybe the butler dressed up in a sheet. But he didn't. He sat, pursed his lips and studied his fingernails.

"You're right," he said, surprisingly. "Did you get all your equipment set up this afternoon?"

"You should see it," said Emily. "He has two huge tripods, each with a special camera at the top of it. We've locked the cameras up in the truck in case someone pinches them, and we'll bring them back when they're needed. Then he has a gigantic white umbrella which directs special light humans can't see into the area where the cameras are pointing."

"Ultraviolet light," said Sean. "It attracts entities."

"I see," said Oscar.

"And he has an ambient temperature measuring device," continued Emily. "Apparently, when entities are present, the temperature drops slightly, and the device can detect this."

"You're learning fast," said Sean. "And finally, I have my EMF scanner. I ran it over the area we're focusing on, or the residual haunting location, as we call it in the trade, and I detected background evidence of recent paranormal anomalies. Spill-through, we call that."

"It was so exciting," said Emily. "I forgot to be scared."

"In that case," said Oscar, "seeing as you're all ready to go, I suppose we should head to the ruins and be in position before nightfall. Although, like most stakeouts, we may find tonight's exercise comprises several hours of waiting for nothing."

"There are no guarantees," said Sean. "But I have had considerable success in the past."

"One other question before we dash off," said Oscar. "What will we do with the ghost once we've caught it?"

"We haven't been asked to catch it," I said. "Only to identify it. That's the outcome Lady Dulvington wants."

"So if we discover tonight that it's a teenager in a sheet with a scary foghorn, we'll tell Lady Dulvington, and that'll be the end of the matter?"

"I suppose so. And if we discover it's the restless soul of someone who died here two hundred years ago, we'll tell her that too."

"Then what will she do?" asked Emily.

"She'll call the cavalry. Lady Dulvington's consulted the Church of England."

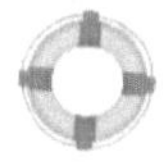

"Ssh," said Emily. "We don't want the entity to know we're here."

Dusk was well advanced as we stepped out of Sean's truck and crept towards the ruins of Alnchurch Park. Emily helped Sean carry his cameras, and they exchanged sideways glances and smiles. He seemed a nice enough chap, if a little eccentric. And that could be said about any of us.

We found Sean's equipment set up in the space which once was the entrance hall, inside the front door facing where the grand staircase would have stood. He tugged two expensive looking digital cameras out of their cases and mounted them on top of the tripods. The cameras pointed towards the rear of the ruins, and the giant umbrella was on a stand between them. I had seen a very similar setup on modelling shoots.

"Careful," said Oscar. "Don't trip over the stones."

"You can shine your phone torches now," said Sean. "But once we're in position, it's best to switch them off to preserve your night vision. You won't be able to see the ultraviolet light; it's above the human visible spectrum."

I perched on a wall which, before the war, would have separated the hall from the dining room. I wondered which lords and ladies had passed through here, attending gala balls, dancing and similar functions. Elizabeth I had stayed here, apparently, five hundred years previously. An unimaginable span of time.

I watched as Oscar took a seat opposite me on another wall, which would have separated the grand hall from the main living areas. His apparent transformation from a vehement sceptic to respecting Sean's expressions and explanations was quite unlike the Oscar I knew and loved, and I wondered whether he was just being polite, or whether he had another trick up his sleeve. I could never tell with him. Sometimes he shared his information; sometimes he played his cards close to his chest.

But the biggest shift in attitude was Emily's. She was terrified of spiders, for goodness' sake. She'd always maintained she was frightened of anything supernatural, and she had a strong belief in ghosts and ghouls, witches and goblins. Yet here she was, poised behind one of Sean's cameras while he looked through the other one, ready to snap a picture of an actual ghost. Or entity, as we now had to call them. I shook my head at her. This wasn't the Emily I knew and loved, either. What was going on?

"Everybody, it's almost dark," said Sean in a stage whisper. "Keep quiet and still, please. I'm going to switch on the ultraviolet light, the ambient temperature measuring device and my EMF scanner, and we'll wait for any paranormal activities to occur. And don't be surprised if there aren't any tonight. Often it takes several nights of stakeouts to achieve a PSI hit, using Kirlian photography."

"PSI hit," whispered Oscar to himself. "Kirlian photography." He shook his head and shrugged.

Sean reached behind the white umbrella, and we heard the click of a switch.

"Does it work on batteries?" asked Emily.

"Yes. Rechargeable lithium ones. It doesn't take much power to produce enough ultraviolet to attract entities. They'll last all night."

"I hope we're not here all night. This is fascinating, but I have to be up at five."

"Nothing changed when you switched that on," I said.

Sean turned to me. "Correct," he said, quietly. "Humans can't see ultraviolet. But I assure you, if there's an entity here, it'll be wondering what we're up to."

"I can't work out whether I'm excited or scared," whispered Emily.

"Shh," said Sean. "Be as quiet as you can. Then we'll have more chance of seeing something."

I shuffled my backside, which was becoming cold on the wall, and made a mental note to bring a blanket to sit on if we repeated the exercise. If Sean's predictions were correct, we might need to return multiple times.

We waited, motionless. An owl hooted.

"What was that?" hissed Emily.

"An owl," said Oscar. "Maybe it'll fly past and we'll be able to decide if it resembles a ghost."

Nothing flew past. The owl hooted again, and we heard the flap of a bird's wings nearby. Or maybe it was a bat. I decided not to tell Emily about this possibility.

Emily and Sean stood still, gazing above their respective cameras at the view the lenses would have. Sean waved his scanner around and studied the screen of his temperature measuring device.

No ghosts, or entities, made themselves known.

I checked my phone. An hour had passed since we'd begun.

"This is boring," whispered Emily. "I wish these ghosts would hurry."

I laughed at her. "Last week you didn't want to see one; now you can't wait for one to pop out."

"Shh," said Sean. "If there's going to be any chance of seeing an entity tonight, we have to be silent."

My backside, I was convinced, had frostbite by now. I tried to tug my coat further beneath it.

A light breeze rustled the trees as we continued our vigil.

"What time is it now?" whispered Emily.

I checked my phone. "Just past eleven o'clock. We've been here two hours."

Emily sighed. "Sorry, Sean. I can't stay awake any longer. Could you give me a ride back to my car? I'll come back another night, I promise."

"I understand," he said. "Shiraz, Oscar, keep watch. Silently, if possible. I'll drop Emily at the gatehouse, then return."

They shone their phone torches at the ground and stepped over the stones, exiting the ruins. I heard the click of the truck's doors unlocking.

HAWWWWWWWWWOOOOOOOOOOOOOOOOOOO

My hair felt like it was standing on end. I jumped to my feet and completely forgot about being quiet.

"Sean, Emily, come back. Quick. Ghost. Entity. Whatever. It's here. Now."

CHAPTER SIXTEEN

"Did you hear it?" I asked Sean, as he sprinted back towards us.

"How could we miss it?" said Emily, following him closely. She gripped Sean's arm, and her body trembled. "I'm torn between needing to run away as fast as I can and wanting to see whatever made that noise."

"I don't notice any mischievous teenagers," Sean said to Oscar, raising his eyebrows. "Do you?"

"I don't see anything," said Oscar, gazing around in the gloom. "I'm trying to work out which direction the noise came from." He took one step forward. "It would be very useful if whatever made the sound repeated it." He turned to Sean. "I'm going to switch on my torch."

"If you do, we've less chance of attracting the ghost. And we know it's present."

"I understand, but bear with me. We heard the noise, and we know whatever made it is close by, right, Shiraz?"

"Definitely. The noise surrounded us, as if we were standing between multiple speakers at a rock concert."

"Sean, please let me rule out once and for all my theory that this is a person. If we search the ruins for anything natural, such as a human with a megaphone, and we don't find one, I'll be more inclined to go along with your supernatural theory."

"It could still be hares or other animals," I said.

"Did that sound like an animal noise to you?" asked Oscar.

"No, but I'm no expert on the sounds hares make."

"Let's at least rule out human-created sounds. Ready, everyone?"

"If you must," said Sean.

We covered our eyes as Oscar's torch threw a beam onto the rear wall of the main hall where we stood.

"We'll search room by room again," he said. "Switch on your phone lights and be careful not to trip. If anyone sees anything man-made, however insignificant, call it out. Start in the room to our left. The old dining room."

I crept around the perimeter of the dining room, shining my phone at every low wall which marked the layout of the ruined house. I checked everywhere where someone could have been hiding. Oscar circumnavigated the room in the opposite direction, while Sean and Emily combed the floor in the centre.

"Anything?" asked Oscar once we'd rendezvoused on the far side.

"Nothing. No people, and no loudspeakers or anything similar."

"Next room," said Oscar. "The living room and ballroom on the opposite side of the hall."

We repeated the process with both these rooms with the same result.

"I really have to go," said Emily. "I'm so tired, I can hardly stand up."

"We'll all leave," said Oscar, "once we've checked the main hall and staircase."

We returned to the room where Sean's equipment was set up near the front entrance. To the rear, where the main staircase was originally located, the walls were higher and more solid. Oscar checked them inside and out. He inspected every gap with his torch, then stood back and illuminated the entire rear wall. It stood several feet high and was the most intact.

"The Elizabethans knew how to build walls, didn't they?" said Oscar. "This part, where the staircase would've been, is probably the oldest part of the building. At the top of the wall, you can see the remains of slits where soldiers would have fired arrows when an enemy was approaching."

"The walls here are very thick," I said. "I suppose to fortify them against cannons, or whatever attacked stately homes in those days. It really is an absolute tragedy all this history has been lost by the bombing."

"Yes. It doesn't bring us any nearer to identifying the source of the noise. At least we can rule out humans. Nobody's here, and we haven't found any sign of anything that could've produced that sound."

"I conclude it was an entity," said Sean. "We've recorded a PSI hit."

"You can call it that if you like," said Oscar. "I'm simply saying it wasn't a person."

"Please take me home," said Emily. "I'm only going to get five hours sleep now. I'll need a nap tomorrow afternoon."

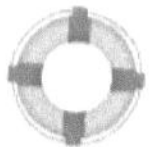

I woke very late the following morning. Rain had started during the night, and it drummed on the roof of the barge. I loved that feeling of being cosy and warm, snuggled under my covers while the weather did its worst outside. And when the wind blew, the boat rocked gently, like a mother would rock a baby's cradle. The effect was identical, and I'd never slept so well. Better than I had at Emily's flat, when the window rattled in a strong southerly. Now I had no trouble sleeping. Finding the motivation to get up was a bigger challenge.

But now, at almost eleven o'clock in the morning, I needed to. Because if I didn't consume at least one double shot skinny latte fairly immediately, I would probably die. At least, that's what my body was threatening me with. I poked an experimental toe out of the covers. The heating had been on all morning, and my toe didn't freeze off, so I followed it with my legs and then my whole body. I sat on the bed and stretched.

In my old life in London, getting to bed after midnight was a nightly occurrence. Often, at the witching hour, I was between engagements, on my way to another nightclub or post-event party. Sometimes I attended four different celebrations in one night, and rising during the afternoon to do the whole thing again was completely unremarkable. These days, I never saw midnight, so last night had been very unusual.

Poor Emily. I hoped she'd woken to open the café in time.

Not least because if she hadn't, and my regulation coffee wasn't provided to me instantly, I couldn't be responsible for my actions.

I threw on yesterday's clothes, covered my bed hair in a beanie hat and chose a full-length raincoat from my wardrobe. The hat and coat didn't match, which was a cardinal sin, and I glanced at the closed door of my spare bedroom. I really needed to make a start on that.

Immediately.

Today.

After coffee.

I slipped on some shoes and ascended the steps.

The rain formed huge puddles along the harbour wall, and I strode as fast as I could, dodging between them. The commercial fishing fleet, I noted, was out to sea at the moment, and the pleasure boats and day tripping craft rocked at their moorings. Ropes against the masts of sailing boats ding-ding-dinged rhythmically, making a pleasing, nautical background noise. The marine rescue shed stood locked and shuttered, and I remembered we had night training scheduled for this evening, which I presumed Murph would cancel in today's gale. I turned the handle of the Wicked Whelk's door and entered a haven from the storm.

"Morning, Shiraz," said Emily. "I can almost say, 'Good Afternoon,' you lucky thing. I'm running on the whiff of an oily rag. Two more hours until closing, and I can lie down before training tonight. Could I get you your double shot skinny latte?"

"Yes, please. Make it a supersize one. I'm desperate."

"Hi, Shiraz," said a voice from one of the tables.

I turned around and met eyes with Sean. "Hello, Sean. Have you come in for brunch?"

"Sean's been recapping last night with me," said Emily. "It's been great, to be honest. He's been here since opening, and it's helped me stay awake."

I lowered my voice. "Is this the start of something new, Emily? You seem to be spending a lot of time together."

"Who knows? I enjoy his company. And I think he enjoys mine. He's talked to me about joining his business and learning from him."

"Really? But what about the Wicked Whelk? You can't abandon it. How would I get my morning coffee, apart from anything else?"

"Don't worry, Shiraz. It's early days. Very early days. Here's your drink."

"Thanks." I took an urgent sip almost before it had left her hand and beamed as I felt the caffeine course through my veins. I idly thought of Lady Dulvington's errant son, in and out of rehab for alcoholism and wondered if there was a similar program for coffee addicts. But why would there be? Who'd want to give up coffee?

I sat opposite Sean. "Hi," I said. "Were you up early as well?"

"I always survive on five hours sleep per night. My body doesn't need more. So when I woke this morning at my usual time, I thought I'd pop down to see Emily." He leant towards me. "You used to live with her, right?"

"Yes. For the first four months of the year, I stayed in her flat upstairs. Why?"

"What's she like to live with? What does she enjoy?"

"Books, mainly. And cats. She's an introvert and prefers the company of one or two close friends. She hates crowds or being the centre of attention. Unlike me. I've spent my life in the lens of a camera."

"Oh? Tell me more."

"I used to be a model, and I was married to a well-known society man in London. My life was a constant whirlwind of film premieres, parties and fashion parades."

"So why are you here?"

"I didn't want that life anymore. And the catalyst for getting out was discovering my husband's affair with his personal assistant. That's why I came to Redcliff and ended up with Emily."

"Emily." His mouth formed a silly grin, and his eyes took on a faraway expression. "D'you know if she's seeing anyone at the moment?"

"She hasn't had a relationship since I've known her. She had a mutual attraction to another member of our marine rescue crew, but neither of them seems to have the courage to take it any further."

"Would you put in a good word for me?"

"Um, sure, but I don't know you any better than she does. You're a nice chap, and you're obviously educated about your chosen career, but…"

"That'll do," said Sean. "Tell her exactly what you just said. I'm a nice chap and educated about my chosen career."

"Okay, I'll talk to her. But only because I think it'll be good for her to get out and meet more people. Not because I believe you're Prince Charming. That's up to you to convince her."

"Thanks, Shiraz. Shh. Here she comes."

"Are we all done here?" asked Emily, collecting our cups.

"Could I get a second cup as a takeaway?" I asked. "At the very least, I have to open the door to my spare room today and estimate the size of the task. And I'll see you at marine rescue training tonight, if Murph doesn't cancel it in this weather."

"After I've had a nap," said Emily. "One hour, thirty-five minutes to go until closing." She forced her eyes open and walked back to the counter.

"Sean," I said. "We need a debrief about last night. Are you free this afternoon? I'll ask Oscar to pop around too. Maybe three o'clock?"

"Certainly," he said. He lowered his voice. "And don't forget what I said about Emily."

"I won't. See you later on."

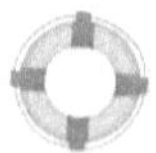

Oscar and Sean sat opposite each other at my dining table, facing off as if they were opponents in a game of chess. Although Oscar had been more accepting of Sean's paranormal qualifications at the stakeout the previous night, I'd have been surprised if he hadn't still retained a healthy level of scepticism. Oscar took nothing at face value. Any person, any clue, any event, Oscar always wanted to dig deeper before jumping to conclusions.

And I wondered what he'd concluded about the wailing sound.

I placed three cups of tea on the table. Generally, at that point, I'd have reached my catering limits, but as Emily wasn't present, I'd bought a plastic-wrapped Madeira cake from the Redcliff store. She'd never have approved of me serving mass-produced refreshments, so we needed to ensure we finished it and disposed of the evidence. I sliced it into nine pieces and hoped we could consume three each. I sat between the two opponents and waited for the first one to make a move.

Oscar cupped his hands around his tea and leant forwards towards Sean. "What's your explanation for the sound we heard, Sean? I had originally believed it to be animals, but now we've heard it considerably closer, I'm undecided."

"It's not an animal sound," said Sean. "Or a human one. I'm convinced it's an ADC."

"ADC?" asked Oscar. "The only thing I'm aware those initials stand for is Assistant District Commissioner."

"After Death Communication," said Sean. "A message from beyond the grave. I believe we're seeing a classic case of AP, or Area Possession, where one or more entities occupy a physical space."

"You seem convinced it's paranormal, to use your own terminology. What about you, Shiraz?"

"I also don't believe it's animals or humans. The noise seemed to emanate from the very house itself. Even though it's a ruin, it's like it was echoing. An echo of the house's former glory, to coin a phrase?"

"I hadn't considered that," said Sean. "The noise being made by an inanimate object, namely the destroyed building. That would be very interesting. I must do more research. I'll contact colleagues in the profession and see if anyone's experienced similar PSI hits."

"That wasn't what I meant," I said. "I didn't mean the house was making the noise. I meant it emanated from within the house. Even though the house is no longer there. Am I making sense?"

"You believe there are anomalous phenomena buried in the old walls?" asked Sean. "Even though most of the walls no longer exist?"

"Yes, or maybe in the remains of the walls. The only word I can use to describe the sound was 'omnipresent', like it was coming from everywhere at once. Like a rock concert. Have you ever been to a huge, stadium concert? And when the band starts playing, the sound comes from all around? That's what I mean."

"I have to admit, I agree," said Oscar, leaning back. "It was like being at the cinema, when there's a dramatic moment in the film."

"In which case, this definitely wasn't made by a human or animal," said Sean. "It was anomalous. Now we have to find out which entity is creating the sound and why. Nothing showed up on any of my equipment."

"Let me grab the investigation sheet," I said. "Move your drinks."

Oscar and Sean lifted their cups off the table, and I shifted the plate of cake. The investigation sheet lay rolled up on the couch, and I rolled it the other way to flatten it, then laid it out on the table between them.

"As we've concluded the noise is supernatural," I said, "we can discount every suspect, sorry, candidate, on the left side." I poised the marker, ready to cross out the names of living people.

"Not so fast," said Oscar. "Give them a low score, like we did in the other investigations. We may need to return to them once we uncover more evidence."

"Got it." I wrote '1' next to the names of Lady Dulvington, Barrowman, Stokes, Jennings and Lucas, the wayward son. "Right, candidates who aren't living. Lady Dulvington's birth mother. She would still seem to be the most likely suspect. Somebody who was in torment at the time of death; she had a personal tragedy in the location of the wailing, and...and...oh! I've had a revelation."

CHAPTER SEVENTEEN

"What revelation have you had, Shiraz?" asked Oscar. The corners of his mouth turned up.

"Lady Dulvington, Barrowman and Jennings all saw a figure in white, correct?"

Oscar nodded. "So they say."

"Lady Dulvington's mother was a nurse, her father's nurse. Nurses wear white uniforms, don't they? I think the apparition was Lady Dulvington's mother."

"Of course," said Sean. "An apparitional experience of a nurse. That's the most likely explanation. If we can persuade her to reappear using the ultraviolet light, perhaps we can capture her on one of the cameras with Kirlian photography."

"You mentioned that phrase at the first stakeout," said Oscar. "What is Kirlian photography?"

"Kirlian photography is named after a man called Seymon Kirlian. It's a technique used to photograph paranormal entities. It can also photograph people's auras, or even a fetch."

"Fetch?" asked Oscar.

"An entity of a living person," said Sean. "Sometimes called a Doppelgänger. A person currently living is actually the entity, but they're elsewhere at the time."

"That would be where the two sides of our investigation sheet cross over," I said. "D'you think this situation is likely, Sean?"

"Set that aside for now," said Sean. "Fetches are rare in residual hauntings. That expression means repetitive paranormal activity in the same place."

"I'm impressed by how knowledgeable you are about your subject," said Oscar. "There's a lot more to the ghost hunting business than I imagined."

"Paranormal investigations, Oscar, please."

"Shall I give Lady Dulvington's mother a score of nine?" I asked.

"I think so," said Oscar. "Given her state at the time of death, the manner of her death, and the matter of the white outfit, she seems to be the most likely candidate. But I'm not saying, 'Case closed' yet."

"No. Gosh, I miss Emily's contribution. She'll have her head down now after her lost sleep last night."

"I miss her contribution too," said Sean. "She's become very interested in the subject. Extraordinary, given her former achluophobia."

"That's a mouthful," I said. "What does achlo-whatever mean?"

"An excessive and irrational fear of darkness or the night. That's all."

"Why didn't you simply say that?" asked Oscar. "Okay, let's give our remaining subjects a score. I think the workman who fell off the ladder and the housekeeper who perished in the bombings should receive a five. We have no more information about them, and Sister Florrie's parish records are silent on further details. Then there's the noise which scared Lady Dulvington's son when he was a boy and made him terrified of the thought of ghosts for life. I see no connection between it and the current events."

"The footsteps circling in the lane outside Alnchurch Park," I said. "Would you call that an entity, Sean?"

"The entity is the paranormal subject causing the phenomenon. Here, as with the wailing in the ruins, the phenomenon is a sound. Phenomena are most commonly sightings or sounds; more rarely touch or even smell. You may have heard stories about people waking up thinking somebody's sitting on their bed, but when they turn on the light, no one's there. That would be an example of a touch phenomenon. And a colleague of mine has encountered an entity which gave off a smell of daffodils. It transpired the entity was an old lady who wore a daffodil-scented perfume. In that case, the entity was the old lady's spirit, and the phenomenon was the perfume."

"Thank you for that detailed explanation. So the footsteps are a phenomenon, but we don't know what entity caused them?"

"You're catching on," said Sean. "You and Emily will be able to compare notes soon. You're seeing her later, aren't you? Don't forget what we talked about."

"I'll see her at this evening's marine rescue training." I smiled at him. "And, yes. I haven't forgotten."

"Back to the matter in hand," said Oscar. "I don't think we can consider these footsteps. We have no evidence they happened at all beyond a second-hand report from Lady Dulvington which in legal terms would be called hearsay, plus the location is wrong. Lady Dulvington's asked us to identify a ghost in the ruins. Not in the lane outside. Give them a '1', Shiraz."

"Done. So our top candidate is Lady Dulvington's mother, by a long way. With secondary candidates of the workman who fell off the ladder and the housekeeper. How do we narrow this down further?"

"Easy," said Sean. "We perform another stakeout. You mentioned you had training on the rescue boat tonight? How about tomorrow?"

"Perfect. And Emily won't be so concerned about staying up late, as the café's closed on Sundays."

"That reminds me," said Oscar. "Lady Dulvington hasn't yet confirmed if we can interview Lucas on Sunday." He glanced up at my kitchen clock, a brass instrument which must've been one of the original barge fittings. "Four-thirty," he said. "Cadbury needs his walk."

"Cadbury's your dog, Oscar?" asked Sean.

"Yes. Why?"

"Has he ever shown signs of animal PSI? Unexplained reactions to something you can't see?"

"Never. If he barks, I know someone's at the door. He doesn't just bark at mid-air."

"Would you consider bringing him along to the stakeouts? If we notice him suddenly becoming alert, even though nothing's visible, it might indicate an entity's nearby."

"It's more likely to indicate a rabbit's nearby," said Oscar. "I'll think about it."

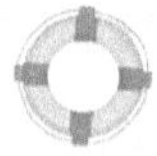

"Gather round, everyone." Murph addressed the team in the marine rescue training room, kitted up in our yellow overalls, ready for an evening on the water. Together with Emily and me, Frances was the qualified crew on tonight's shift and one other recruit, Colin, made up the full complement of five on the boat, which was the maximum before it became cramped. The gale had abated, and a brisk breeze skipped whitecaps across the ocean.

"This evening," continued Murph, "we'll practice the searches we learnt at our last academic session. Who can correctly tell me which ones?"

"Expanding square search and sector search," said Emily. "We also touched on line searches."

"Correct. Colin, describe the theory behind an expanding square search."

"We start at the last known location, or the most likely location, of the missing person, and work our way outwards, turning right ninety degrees after each leg."

"Ye-es," said Murph. "That's roughly correct, although if I catch you calling starboard 'right' tonight, I won't be impressed. Could you draw what you mean on the whiteboard?"

Colin walked to the front of the room, picked up a black marker and drew a pattern.

"Good," said Murph. "Spot on. When's the best time to choose this search pattern?"

"When you only have one boat searching and you know roughly where the person is," said Colin.

"Yes. And the major drawback?"

"If you miss them, you won't cover the same part of the water again."

"Exactly. Well done. Shiraz, please describe a sector search."

"We drop a buoy or fender in the water at the most likely start point. Then the boat describes triangles which constantly go through that spot, past the buoy. That way, we're covering the most likely part multiple times."

"Draw it for me," said Murph.

Colin handed me the marker. I picked up the board rubber, erased his diagram and replaced it with my sector search one, which I liked to think of as the Trivial Pursuit counter search.

"Excellent," said Murph. "What's the problem with this type of search? Anyone?"

We all looked at each other. I knew I was getting better at memorising Murph's pearls of wisdom while forgetting to open my workbook between sessions, but I didn't think we'd covered this question at our academic training. And I was pleased to see my fellow recruits also didn't know.

"Frances?" asked Murph. "You should remember."

"It's the opposite of the drawback of the expanding square. With the expanding square, the area covered is ever-increasing. With the sector search, we're constantly covering the same area. So if the casualty isn't where we thought they were, we might never find them."

"Right," said Murph. "We need to select which search pattern we choose carefully, based on our knowledge of each unique situation. This evening, we'll practice both types of search in the light, then, when it gets dark at around eight-thirty, we'll practice them again. Searching after dark is much harder, but we have multiple additional tools available to us. Hopefully, the main FLIR works tonight and doesn't become stuck pointing at the sky. I've tried to get it fixed, but they don't make that model anymore, and it's on borrowed time until I can buy a new one. Okay, everyone. Let's get the boat in the water."

Frances hopped into the driving seat of the tractor, pulled the boat on its trailer out of the shed, performed a three-point turn and backed it down the boat ramp. I stared open-mouthed in awe of her driving ability. On one memorable occasion, in the middle of the King's Road in Chelsea, I attempted to do a three-point turn in my Porsche when I spotted a vacant parking space on the opposite side of the road outside Anine Bing, one of my favourite clothes stores. I held up the traffic for several minutes in both directions while I performed the manoeuver and, by the time I completed it, someone else had pinched the space. And here Frances was not only doing a three-point turn in two movements, but she had the boat on its trailer behind her as well. I knew reversing the boat was part of the qualified crew training, and I wasn't looking forward to that part of the course.

Murph drove the boat off the trailer and docked it gently against the harbour wall, while Frances returned the tractor and trailer to the shed. We boarded the rescue vessel and selected a lifejacket each. Frances locked the shed and joined us, and we headed out of the harbour mouth for the open sea.

I checked my phone. Seven o'clock. The sun was low in the sky, and the breeze was abating further. The beach was empty of daytrippers, but a few pleasure craft caught the last of the evening light. I watched a group of four small sailing boats tack across the bay, changing direction together as if they were a flock of birds in flight.

"How was your chat with Oscar and Sean?" asked Emily.

"Good. Productive. Did you have a pleasant afternoon nap?"

"Yes, thanks. I caught up on my missed sleep, which is good, as I think we might be out late again tonight."

"Murph said we'll be done by ten. We should meet tomorrow, so I can bring you up to speed on everything at Alnchurch Park. D'you want to pop around after the café closes?"

"Okay. I don't have anything planned."

"Oh, and tomorrow evening, Sean wants to do his next stakeout. He asked Oscar to bring Cadbury, in case the ghost is visible to dogs."

"I've heard of that. Animal PSI."

"Sean said you were an excellent student. He's a nice chap, and he's obviously educated about his chosen career."

I think those were the words Sean asked me to say, verbatim.

"He is, isn't he?" said Emily. She shrugged and showed me her clenched teeth. "I can't wait to see him tomorrow night. He's taught me so much. I'm not as scared anymore, now I understand the subject better."

Murph slowed the engines and brought the marine rescue boat to a stop.

"Okay. Let's imagine we've received a call from Coastguard Headland Bay. They've told us about a missing kayaker, last seen at these co-ordinates. We've arrived here, and we've decided to begin an expanding square search."

"Why have we selected expanding square and not sector?" asked Colin.

"We cover a larger area with an expanding square, remember? A kayak will move faster through the water than a human, as it has a bigger surface area to be blown by the wind or swept along in a current. We'll assume for now that the kayaker is still with their vessel, and we'll practise as if the instruments don't have the automatic search feature. So someone will need to call out the turns to the skipper. Who wants to go first?"

"I will," I said. I figured that if I got this wrong, at least I had the excuse I hadn't seen my colleagues perform the exercise.

"Okay, Shiraz. Draw out your search pattern on the piece of paper and make the first and second legs one minute. To make the maths easy, we'll start on a heading of zero degrees, or due north."

I flipped over the boat log sheet and found a clean piece of paper. Within a minute, I'd drawn the 'snail painted by Picasso' as I named the square spiral, and I wrote '1' on the first two legs, '2' on the second two, '3' on the third two and '4' on the last two. Emily and Colin watched over my shoulders, then I held up the paper to show Murph.

"Spot on," he said. "Ready to start? You'll need your phone as a timer."

I swiped my phone and selected the clock function. Murph nodded as I glanced up at him.

"Everyone holding on?" he said.

"Holding on," we replied in unison.

"Three, two, one, go." I pushed the button to start the timer, and Murph shoved the throttles forward.

We headed in a straight line as I watched the timer count down.

"Give me a five second warning to make the turn," called Murph.

"Five, four, three, two, one, and turn starboard ninety degrees."

The boat swung, and shadows moved as we now headed due east.

"Eyes on the water, everyone," said Murph. "Not on me or Shiraz. We're searching for a kayaker, remember?"

"Five, four, three, two, one, and turn starboard ninety degrees." I repeated, and we swung due south. This leg would be twice as long, as our search area expanded. After two minutes, I called again. "Five, four, three, two, one, and turn starboard ninety degrees."

Murph swung the vessel due west, and we began the next two minute leg.

We continued in this fashion with the legs constantly expanding until we'd completed the search pattern. Murph brought the boat to a stop.

"Debrief, everyone," he said. "What did we learn from that?"

"My biggest learning," I said, "is that when I'm calling instructions to the skipper, I can't take part in the search. That's one less set of eyes on the water."

"Correct," said Murph. "When we're on what I would call a vanilla job, such as towing a boat with a flat battery, we can manage with two people on board, a skipper and a qualified crew. But when we're on a search, there are never enough crew members."

"My eyes became tired," said Colin. "On the last leg, I started to imagine things."

"That's another reason for needing several crew. We have to spell each other, swapping sides of the boat or taking a rest.

It's hard to keep focussed for long. Okay, change places. Emily can call the shots this time, then Colin."

We repeated the exercise twice more and then moved onto the sector search. The process was identical, except we changed direction at a different angle and repeatedly passed a buoy we'd dropped in the water.

"This is boring," whispered Emily, while Colin called the instructions for the sector search.

"As boring as waiting three hours for a ghost to pop out?"

"Of course not. That's fun, the anticipation and not knowing."

"Stop," said Murph. "We'll take a break, then repeat both of those in the dark."

Emily puffed and rolled her eyes.

The radio bursting into life curtailed her lack of enthusiasm.

"Marine Rescue Redcliff, Marine Rescue Redcliff, this is Coastguard Headland Bay. Come in, please. Over."

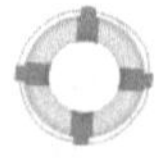

CHAPTER EIGHTEEN

Frances grabbed the handset. "Coastguard Headland Bay, this is Marine Rescue Redcliff receiving. Go ahead. Over."

"We've received a distress call from a fisherman who's fallen out of his boat. We have co-ordinates. Are you ready to take them down? Over."

"Go ahead. Over."

The voice read out numbers which I knew to be latitude and longitude.

Frances noted them and repeated them back into the radio. "Those co-ordinates put him one mile off Golden Beach. Do you have any more information? Over."

"Negative. We've tried calling the number he rang from, but it rings out. We believe he yelled his position before his phone was submersed. Over."

"Received. Marine Rescue Redcliff heading to the location to search for one person in the water. ETA ten minutes. Over."

"Please advise when on scene. Coastguard Headland Bay out."

"Training over," said Murph. "This is a Mayday. Everyone holding on?"

"Holding on," we all responded as he pushed the throttle levers forward.

"All we know is he fell off his boat at those co-ordinates," said Murph. "We don't know whether he was in a kayak, or whether it's an ocean-going yacht. We assume it's one person, but it could be more. We don't know whether he's wearing a lifejacket, how old he is, whether he's fit or not. What can we do to prepare?"

"Fetch blankets and towels," said Emily.

"Yep. Grab them. What else?"

"Make sure we have torches and spotlights ready to search in the water," said Colin.

"Definitely. Grab one of those LED torches each while you have the chance. Anything else?"

"Switch on the radar and FLIR," I said.

"Bingo," said Murph. "It's almost dark now. We have the radar on, and if he's tumbled out of a metal boat, it'll light up. A plastic kayak, not so much. Shiraz, turn the FLIR on. Ask Frances if you can't remember how to do that. Where should we begin our search?"

"Where he entered the water," I said. "As soon as we find his boat."

"Yep. And if we're really lucky, he'll have climbed back on board, and we'll merely need to warm him up."

"FLIR on, skipper," I said, as the square screen in front of me lit up to show a uniformly grey image.

"Grab the hand-held FLIR as well, Shiraz," said Murph. "D'you remember how to use it?"

"Yes. Remember I illuminated the couple kissing on the beach?"

"Ah, yes. How could I forget?"

"Vessel dead ahead on radar," said Frances.

Murph glanced at the radar screen and pulled back the throttles. "Shiraz, keep your eyes on the FLIR screen as we approach. We'll come up slowly; the last thing we want to do is run over the man we're supposed to be saving."

We drifted slowly. Frances watched the radar screen and peered forward. Emily had readied the blankets and towels, and she held a torch out to one side of the rescue boat, sweeping it across the sea. I stared at the screen of the FLIR, which still showed uniformly grey.

"Sidesplitting sea shanties," said Murph, glancing at the image in front of me. "The main FLIR's not working. It's pointing at the sky again." He jabbed his finger upward. "Just when we need it in an actual emergency, it fails completely. Frances, could you try to unjam it?"

"Okay, Murph. Going forward."

"Permission granted," said Murph.

We watched her step around the side of the boat and stand directly in front of us, with her hands tugging at something on the roof of the cabin. The picture on the FLIR screen changed, and Frances returned.

"Fixed it," she said.

"Uh-uh." I tapped the screen as the image reverted to a uniform grey. "It's swung back to point at the sky again."

"Bumbling bar pilots." Murph thumped the dashboard. "The sooner we receive our next large donation, the better. Shiraz, use the hand-held FLIR by itself. That's better than nothing. Okay, folks. Here's the fisherman's boat, dead ahead. Let's check for any sign of him."

We came alongside the small fishing boat.

"Hello?" called Colin. "Anyone here?" He leant over the rails and peered into the tiny cabin.

"It's empty," he said.

Frances plucked the radio handset from its cradle. "Coastguard Headland Bay, this is Marine Rescue Redcliff. Over."

"Marine Rescue Redcliff, this is Coastguard Headland Bay. Go ahead. Over."

"We're on scene, and we've found the vessel. It's empty. Over."

"Commence a search immediately. Marine Rescue Headland Bay will arrive to help as soon as they've finished their current job. And the helicopter's available within twenty minutes. Over."

"Received. Marine Rescue Redcliff commencing a single-vessel search for one POB. Over."

"We'll update you on the ETA of the other assets. Coastguard Headland Bay out."

"We're it," said Murph. "For at least twenty minutes, we're all that's between the missing fisherman and drowning. We'll start a sector search using the empty boat as the central point. Shiraz, hop up on the bow with the hand-held FLIR. Keep it pointed at the sea in front of us. Far enough away so we see him before we hit him. If you need me to turn, hold out an arm to show me which direction. Colin, you and Emily can grab a hand-held spotlight each and search port and starboard. Frances, create a search pattern on the instruments for me to follow."

"Got it, Murph," I said. "Going forward."

"Permission granted."

I nipped up to the bow with the FLIR and stood behind the rails pointing it into the sea. The screen's colour changed as I clicked its background through green to red and then orange, which seemed to offer the best visibility in tonight's conditions. I experimented with pointing it back at Colin and noted he lit up as a white blob. I hoped the fisherman would too.

"Going up. Hold on," yelled Murph.

"Holding on," we all responded, and he increased the rescue vessel's speed to a slow cruise. I presumed this was because we couldn't see far in the dark, and because he had me up on the bow. The elliptical shapes of Emily and Colin's spotlights lit up a section of green sea on either side of the boat. It was a dark night with no moon, and I knew the fisherman would be very lucky if we found him.

"Turning starboard one-twenty," yelled Murph, and I held on as our boat swung around the outer edge of the search area. The FLIR screen still showed the orange waves on the water, but no white blobs. My palm became cold against the boat's rail, and I swapped the FLIR to my other hand. We turned through 120 degrees again and headed back towards our starting point.

"Vessel dead ahead," I yelled, as the fisherman's abandoned craft loomed out of the darkness. Murph passed it close to our starboard side, and we began the second sector of our search.

As we were turning 120 degrees on the far edge of our search area, a white blob lit up on the left-hand side of my screen.

"Stop!" I yelled and held out my left arm. "Turn to port. Slowly."

Frances leant out of the cabin window. "What have you seen?" she asked.

"Something in the water. Slow. Slow. Fifty feet away."

Murph put the engines into neutral, and the rescue boat drifted.

"Shiraz," yelled Frances. "If this is him, as soon as you have visual, hold your arm out straight in that direction. Show us where he is."

"Got it."

"Hey!" I heard a voice from the water. "Help. Over here."

I held my arm out toward the sound. I couldn't see anyone with my naked eyes, but the blob on the FLIR grew larger.

"Slow," I called to Murph. "Crawling speed."

Our forward motion almost ceased as Murph shoved the throttles into reverse and, suddenly, a person floating on their back appeared in the light of Colin's torch.

"Frances, prepare the rear deck to retrieve the man overboard," yelled Murph. "Colin, keep your spotlight on him. Shiraz, stay there and keep your arm pointed at the casualty."

The spotlight lit up a man wearing an inflatable lifejacket which had deflated. He was treading water on his back. His teeth reflected in the torchlight, and he gave me a thumbs up. Immediately, the tension released from my shoulders.

I waved at him and grinned. "Stay there. We'll come to you."

"Permission to open the boarding door," Emily called from the rear deck.

"Granted," said Murph.

"Ten feet off the bow," I yelled from my position up at the nose of the boat.

"I have visual," said Emily. "Five feet, three feet and...we've got him."

I stuffed the portable FLIR in my pocket, hopped down to join my colleagues and, to my surprise, found the man we'd rescued standing on the rear deck, smiling, with a towel and blanket around him. I estimated his age to be around twenty, and he was tall, the same height as me.

"Thanks, guys," he said. "I thought I was done for."

Frances entered the cabin, and I heard her give Coastguard an update on the radio.

"What's your name?" asked Emily.

"Jayden."

"Were you by yourself?"

"Yes."

"All accounted for," said Emily into the cabin. "No one else to find."

"Thanks," said Murph. "Get him inside, keep him warm, and we'll find his boat again."

"I'll give you a safety briefing, then you can sit with us in the cabin," said Emily. She pointed out the hazards on board and showed Jayden to a seat, then we motored slowly until his craft appeared in front of us.

Frances stepped out of the cabin and spoke to me. "Usually, we'd transfer a member of our crew onto that boat, rather than towing it unmanned. But Murph and I are the only people trained to do that, and we're both needed on the rescue vessel for compliance, until you guys pass your qualified crew certificates. We'll tie two lines in a 'Y' shape onto the bollard on its bow, and tow it fairly closely behind us. That way, even though no one's steering it, it should follow us directly without drifting off to the side. We can't do that in a rough sea, but tonight it'll be okay."

"Got it," I said. "What d'you need me to do?"

Frances laughed. "Tie the lines on. You remember your knots, right?"

"Oh. Yes, I do. But could you check them?"

I lashed two ropes onto a bollard mounted on the fisherman's craft. We towed it back to Redcliff Harbour, keeping our speed at around five knots. Frances kept a close eye astern.

"What happened?" I asked Jayden. "How did you end up in the water?"

"I'd almost finished fishing for the evening. Nothing had bitten all night, and I was all ready to pack up and go home. I'd brought most of my rods in when something tugged at the last one. Something big. I grabbed the rod and tried to reel it in. Whatever this fish was on the end of my line, it was very strong. I fought for twenty minutes, then the line went slack. I thought I'd lost the fish, but I looked over the side and, to my surprise, there it was, having a rest. So I quickly found my net, leant over to scoop up my catch, and the next thing I knew, I was in the water with fishing line tangled all around me and the fish starting to fight again and pulling me with it. My first thought was that it would head for the bottom and drag me down, so I fought to untangle myself. By the time I'd got my legs free, I'd lost my rod, my net and the fish, and I couldn't see my boat any more in the darkness. I pulled my phone out of my pocket and pressed the emergency app."

"You were lucky you had that app," said Murph. "It should be the law for everyone to keep that on their phone."

"I know," said Jayden. "I spoke to the emergency operator and read the co-ordinates off the app, then the screen went flickery and died. I started to swim, but have you ever tried to swim in a lifejacket? It's impossible. And the lights on shore confused me. I wasn't sure if I was going the right way. So I lay on my back to conserve energy and hoped someone was coming."

"Very, very lucky," said Murph. "That lifejacket probably saved your life. It kept you afloat until we arrived."

"I watched you search for me," said Jayden. "I saw your lights, and I yelled when you illuminated my boat. Then you chugged off in the other direction, and I thought you'd left me to drown."

"We'd never do that," I said. "We were beginning a search pattern."

"I worked that out when your lights turned, and you began heading back this way. But you were going to miss me again, then you suddenly stopped and headed straight for me. How did you know where I was?"

"Here's how we found you." I showed Jayden the portable FLIR. "As well as your mobile phone and your lifejacket, this little device saved your life tonight."

"What is it?" he asked. "It looks like the scanners we use on boxes in the warehouse where I work."

"It's called a FLIR, which stands for Forward Looking Infra Red. It detects heat. So a person in the water, such as you, shows up as a white blob. That's how we saw you. I was standing up on the bow pointing it at the sea, and you appeared in it."

"Saved by technology," said Jayden. "Emergency apps, and heat-seeking scanners. You guys have all the equipment."

"Coming down," called Murph, as we entered Redcliff Harbour. I gave myself a subtle thumbs up at the achievement of returning another person safely to their loved ones.

CHAPTER NINETEEN

How does anyone know what the weather's unleashing outside before they even open their eyes? When you live on a barge, it's easy. If the boat's swaying gently, you know the wind's blowing. The harbour keeps her safe from the wildest storms, but sneaky waves find their way in and lap rhythmically along her sides. If there's a noise on the roof like somebody dropping a gigantic bag of dried peas, it's pouring. And if you can hear human activity, people chatting, laughing, kids playing, then it's bound to be warm and sunny. Which is what it was today.

I often wondered whether people walking past my boat along the harbour wall knew I was sleeping safely tucked up on board. The fisherfolk and other regular users of the harbour would've done, of course, but did the tourists? On a busy summer's weekend, hundreds would walk past my home on the way to book a fishing trip, or while taking a stroll to blow away the cobwebs. Did they even know my barge was a home? I wondered if I should buy some hardy, saltwater-loving pot plants to adorn the deck. Although, plastic ones would be the best. My record at keeping plants alive was equal to my record of producing delicious meals from raw ingredients.

Nil.

I jumped at the sight of Boots, the orange cat, lying at the end of my bed. "Hello," I said. "What are you doing there? You don't live here."

He yawned so widely I thought his jaw would dislocate, and he stretched out with his toes splayed.

"You must have come in through the bathroom window again," I said. "Don't make it a habit. I don't keep any cat food here."

The long, kaftan-like robe I used as a dressing gown hung behind my cabin door, and I lifted it down and threw it around myself. I'd have to get dressed to walk over to the Wicked Whelk for a takeaway coffee, but I really needed some new clothes to avoid wearing the same nine outfits repeatedly. I stared at the door of the spare room where piles of unopened cases hid and decided coffee came first. Yesterday's clothes would do for the stroll around the harbour to see Emily. Hopefully, no one who'd seen me yesterday would see me today. Apart from her.

I pulled a cap over my head and threw on a coat. As I unlocked the wheelhouse door, stepped onto my deck and plopped Boots onto the harbour wall, the marine rescue boat cruised past with Murph, Jules, the qualified crew and the new chap called Paul on board. I waved to them, and my smile reached my eyes as they waved back. The words 'Morning, Shiraz,' floated across the water.

This is home. People recognise me. They wave to me. I love that feeling.

I stepped onto the dock and spun around with my arms outstretched.

"Hi," I called out as I opened the door to the café. Emily stood behind the counter, and I was surprised to see Sean in an apron clearing tables. I waved to him.

"Usual double shot skinny latte?" asked Emily once I'd reached the coffee ordering spot.

"Of course.' I pointed my thumb subtly behind me. "New staff member?"

"He offered to help, and I agreed. Just on Saturday mornings when we're flat out with young families." She tamped down the coffee, and the machine hissed.

"But he's only here in Redcliff until we conclude our ghost business," I said. "It might be all over in a week."

"He said I might persuade him to stay on. He likes it here. And...and I like him being here."

"That's lovely. Is he working for free?"

"He's getting coffee and breakfast. I don't want him to think I'm taking advantage."

"Good move. Hey, are you busy this afternoon? You don't have any plans with Sean?"

"He wants to get ready for tonight's stakeout. He has some research to do on the Internet, apparently."

"I wonder what research that could be? Anyway, would you give me a hand? My spare room's crammed to the ceiling, not only with the suitcases Monty sent from London but also some junk the last owner hid in there. Like me, he used it as a dumping ground. Would you give me a hand sorting it out? I can't face the task by myself, and I keep putting it off."

"Okay. Three o'clock, after I've closed up? Here's your coffee."

"Thanks," I said. "I'll see you then." I turned around. "Bye, Sean. See you tonight for some paranormal investigation."

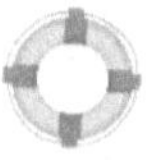

"I see what you mean," said Emily that afternoon, as she studied the piles of bags and boxes stuffed into the spare cabin. "Where are you going to keep everything permanently? And how did it get here?"

"When I moved down here from London last New Year, I only brought with me what I could carry in the taxi. Once I knew I'd have my own place, I sent Monty a shopping list of possessions and asked him to ship them down. His response was to send absolutely everything. There are clothes in here I'd forgotten I owned, and I'm sure not all of them are mine. These shoes, for instance." I picked up a pair of white platform heels. "I've never seen these. Where on earth did they come from?" I tried one on. "They're too small for me. They'd probably fit you."

"I never wear heels."

"Maybe you will for a special occasion one day?"

"Maybe. Um, Shiraz? Could I ask you something?"

"Of course. What's wrong? Why are you biting your nails? This isn't about the ghost, is it?"

"Not directly." She clenched her teeth and sucked in a breath. "Shiraz, I'm worried things are going too fast with Sean."

"Too fast? What's going too fast?"

"I mean, he's good company and very intelligent. But it's been years since I've had anything I could call a relationship, and I'm scared of getting it all wrong and frightening him off."

"You won't," I said. "He likes you too."

"He does? How d'you know that?"

"He told me. In the café. He asked me to put in a good word for him."

"Really?"

"Yes, really. Just be yourself and let whatever might happen, happen."

"You make it sound so straightforward." She sucked in a deep breath then released it. "Okay. Your muddle now. Here's what we'll do. We'll pull all the boxes and cases out and empty them into piles. One pile will be all the clothes you want to keep, one pile for those you could send to a charity shop or give away and another pile for any clothes which have to be ditched.

Then we'll look at how much is left in the 'keep' pile and see if we can find homes for it all in your cupboards."

"What about a pile for clothes you want? Like these heels?"

"I don't want them, Shiraz. I'd never wear them. They can go to the charity shop."

"Maybe Sean would like you in high heels?"

"D'you think so?"

"I'm joking, Emily. But if I take everything to the charity shop, it'll feel funny strolling around Redcliff and seeing other ladies wearing my old clothes."

"Will you even know if they're yours? Pass me the first case."

We emptied eight suitcases, four holdalls, six packing crates, seven hat boxes and several bin bags, some of which split and distributed their contents over the floor. By the time we'd moved all the possessions into my living room, it resembled Selfridge's shop floor during a particularly violent moment of the Boxing Day sales. The couch had completely disappeared under dresses, tops and trousers, the dining table looked like Harrod's hat display the day before Royal Ascot Ladies' Day horse race, and rows of shoes lined the kitchen counter.

I shook my head. "Where do we start?"

"Start at one end and work towards the other. First item. What d'you want to do with this?" She held up a long, soldier-red gown which I'd last worn to a gala ball in Leicester Square the previous year.

"I don't know, Emily. When would I ever wear that in Redcliff? When would I ever wear any of this stuff? I'd look completely out of place."

I sat on the floor and held my head in my hands.

Emily laid the dress down, sat beside me and put her arm around my shoulders.

"I feel completely overwhelmed," I said. "I've managed without all these clothes since New Year. If I go out for a walk, could you make them go away while I'm gone?"

"You don't want any of them?"

My eyes watered, and I returned her hug. "No. Yes. No. I don't know."

Emily stood and held my hands. "Up you get. Your storage problem's given me a great idea. I can make all of this go away, and we'll need to stuff it back in your spare room for now. But you have to be sure you don't want it."

I tugged on her arms and pulled myself up, then stared at the piles of clothes, sighed and made a decision. "I don't want it. Any of it. Make it vanish, Emily."

"Okay, let's stuff it all back in the boxes. It'll be gone by tomorrow. Keep the door closed until then."

"Really?"

"I just need to check with Murph first."

"Murph? What would he want with Gucci dresses and Jimmy Choo high heels? No, don't answer that. I've just had an awful vision."

"Don't ask any more questions. This is going to be amazing. I can't wait."

"Right. Tell me when you feel ready. What about the other things? The stuff which was on the barge from before?" We poked our noses around the spare cabin door and looked at the pile of junk stored there, most of which seemed to be boxes of spare parts for boat engines. A large net on a pole leant against the back wall, and Emily picked it up.

"What's this?" she asked.

"I think it's for catching butterflies. It's too big to be a fishing net, and I reckon the pole wouldn't be strong enough."

"What are you going to do with it?"

"I was going to put it in the rubbish. Whatever you're doing with the dresses and shoes, could it go too?"

"Leave it there for now. I'll need to think about it."

"What, exactly, will be different about tonight?" asked Oscar, taking the same seat on the low wall as he had previously.

"Possibly nothing," said Sean. "We know something's here because of the inhuman, anomalous wailing noise. But entities don't appear on cue. Paranormal investigators can't make appointments with them. They come and go when they want, and a lot of time is spent waiting for something to happen."

"It's surprising how similar our professions are," said Oscar. "In the police, we often waited for hours for a suspect to make an appearance. And then we weren't sure what they'd do."

"I thought you were going to bring your dog tonight? If there is any paranormal activity, he may well see it before we do."

"I'm more interested in what your instruments detect, so I elected to leave him at home."

"Sean," I said. "Emily mentioned you had some research to do before tonight. What did you find out?"

"Something very important. I studied old maps of South West England dating back to medieval times. And I discovered Alnchurch Park is on an ancient ley line."

"Sean showed me the website," said Emily. "It shows imaginary lines connecting old buildings."

"Not so imaginary," said Sean. "A ley line is a line of energy or magic. Stonehenge, for instance, is at the junction of multiple ley lines, as are many of England's historical churches and even Canterbury Cathedral."

"I always thought ley lines were pagan," said Oscar.

"You'd be surprised where paganism and Christianity overlap," said Sean. "The festival we think of as Christmas, December 25th, is, in fact, a pagan festival celebrating midwinter."

"What purely pagan festivals are there?" asked Emily.

"Halloween, or Samhain, to give it its pagan name, is the main one, but, again, it appears in the Christian calendar as All Hallows Eve. The other important one is May Day, when pagans celebrate new birth, and Walpurgis. Walpurgis occurred on April 30th, two weeks ago. It's another opportunity the dead have to revisit the living world."

"That was roughly when the haunting started," I said. "D'you think the entity's come alive because of Walpurgis?"

"Who knows?" Sean laughed. "We'll ask it when we catch it. Okay, everyone, it's almost dark. Silence please, and I'll switch on the ultraviolet."

"Should we spread out?" I asked. "So if the noise begins again, one of us might be closer to it."

"I don't think it would be any help. It felt like the auditory phenomenon was omnipresent, to use a word someone said on Thursday evening."

I sat on the low wall again and watched as Sean took up station behind one camera and directed Emily to stand behind the other. He clicked a switch behind the enormous umbrella.

"Okay," he whispered. "The ultraviolet's on. Quiet, please. Tonight, let's catch an entity."

We waited. Not a breath of wind stirred in the surrounding trees. Night birds twittered in the distance.

Nothing happened.

I tapped my fingers and glanced around in the starlight. My faith was very weak that we'd catch a ghost, although the wailing noise seemed to indicate something supernatural was happening. Or something unexplained, anyway. But we hadn't seen the white phantom at all.

"Something's shown up on the camera," said Sean. "Look."

My scalp prickled, and I walked over to him. If he'd really caught an image of a ghost, I was only feet away from it. It could be standing next to me now. Emily sidled up behind me. I guessed she didn't want to appear nervous in front of Sean.

He showed us the screen on the back of the camera. "The camera caught this picture. It looks like an amorphous spirit."

"It looks like a blob of putty," said Oscar.

"Whatever it resembles, the image was in the viewfinder's range. I believe it to be an orb."

"An orb?" I asked.

"Yes. An unexplained object floating above the ground."

"Was it what Lady Dulvington and the butler saw? I suppose you could mistake it for a person at a distance."

"Orbs change shape frequently," said Sean. "They could form the image of a person."

"Where is it now?" asked Emily, glancing all around. "It could be next to me." She grabbed Sean's arm.

"I think it's gone," he said. "The instruments aren't picking anything up now."

"At least it's not accompanied by that awful howling," I said.

"I hear something," whispered Emily.

I stood and turned my head to the left and the right. "It sounds like an engine."

Oscar jumped up and pointed behind us. "That's not a ghost," he said. "It's a car."

We stared towards the track leading from the gatehouse. Dim headlights meandered across the valley and began the journey up the hill. We heard gravel crunch, then the vehicle parked behind Sean's truck.

"Do entities drive cars?" asked Emily.

"That would be a new PSI hit for me if they did," said Sean. "Or it could be psychokinesis. Movement of physical objects without the use of physical means."

"Shh," I said. "Footsteps. Someone's coming."

We heard a twig snap and indistinct male voices.

Emily clutched Sean's arm. "It's the ghost," she said. "Protect me." She hid behind him and peered around his body.

The sound of the footsteps approached through the trees. We all turned to face them, then I threw my arm over my face as bright torchlight washed over us.

"Good evening," said a voice which sounded very like Redcliff policeman Sergeant Will Bishopstone. "What's going on here?"

CHAPTER TWENTY

"We're looking for a Mr Jake Robinson," said Sergeant Will. Constable Lachlan stood alongside him, shining the torch in our direction, although thankfully he'd stopped pointing it directly in our eyes. Constable Bert puffed up the slope behind them.

I frowned. Emily held Sean's arm. The only one of us who bore any kind of relaxed expression was Oscar.

Sergeant Will held up a photograph and shone his torch at it. He then pointed the light at Sean and nodded.

"Mr Jake Robinson. Also known as Tony Crago. Also known as Philip Johnson. And now, apparently, known as Sean Plumtree. I am arresting you on suspicion of fraud. You do not have to say anything unless you wish to do so, but anything you do say will be taken down and may be given in evidence."

Sean darted his eyes around in the lights of the policemen's torches, tugged his arm away from Emily's grip, turned around and sprinted. As he leapfrogged the low wall Oscar sat on, Oscar grabbed one of his legs, and Sean fell to the ground, clutching his ankle. I covered my mouth. Emily yelped.

Oscar grinned while Sergeant Will tugged out a pair of handcuffs, pulled Sean's arms behind his back and clasped the cuffs around his wrists. He helped him to his feet.

"Constable Bert," he said, "please bring Mr Robinson's possessions and label them. Constable Lachlan, relieve Mr Robinson of the keys to his vehicle and drive his truck to the police station."

"No!" yelled Emily. "You're wrong. He's not Jake Robinson. You've got the wrong guy. Sean's a professional, certified paranormal investigator. Show them your credentials, Sean. Show them your university degree."

Sean met her eyes, then looked down at the ground. She stood still with her mouth open.

He raised his head again and stared at her. "I'm sorry, Emily," he said.

Emily burst into tears, and I held her while Sergeant Will marched Sean away. Lachlan and Bert folded the two tripods and the umbrella. They carted them down to the waiting police vehicle.

"What just happened?" Emily asked me, her eyes wide.

"The police arrested Sean," I said. "Who may not have been called Sean. And it seems he also may not have been who he claimed to be."

"But he knew everything about the supernatural. This is all a mistake. They must have the wrong person."

"They don't," said Oscar. "The man you know as Sean Plumtree is a confidence trickster."

Emily's face reddened, and she stepped towards Oscar with her nostrils flared. "Did you summon the police, Oscar? Did you have Sean arrested? Why? He's not a confidence trickster. He has a degree in parapsychology. I saw the certificate. You're all wrong about him." She wailed, and I threw my arms around her again, but she wriggled and pushed me away.

"Jake Robinson's been conning elderly people for years," said Oscar. "Lady Dulvington already paid him five thousand pounds as a deposit, and she's spent money on his accommodation too. I knew something wasn't right about him, so I did some investigating of my own. And I appear to have saved her the fifteen thousand pound balance."

"But…" said Emily. She bawled again.

"Emily," I said. "I know it's hard, but you should thank Oscar. You don't want a boyfriend who's a professional conman. If he's capable of stealing thousands from elderly people, imagine what he might've stolen from you."

"He stole my heart," said Emily. "That's all he stole from me." She sobbed, and I held her tightly.

I woke on Sunday morning and gently drew back the covers so as not to wake Emily. She was so upset; she hadn't wanted to stay in her flat by herself, but after Oscar had arranged for his taxi friend to bring us back from Alnchurch, she wanted to stay awake until the early hours telling me how much she knew Sean was a good person. She'd refused to speak to Oscar in the car, and I felt so upset for her, but I was convinced she'd had a lucky escape. Emily had finally fallen asleep at four in the morning, and now it was eleven-thirty, which was late rising even for me these days. I threw on my dressing gown and opened the bedroom door quietly. On Sundays, I had to make do with a dreaded homemade coffee, so I boiled my new kettle and spooned coffee granules into a cup. The water began to bubble, and I was about to close the bedroom door to avoid Emily being disturbed when someone knocked from outside.

"Murph," I said, as I opened the door. "What brings you here? Sorry I look such a state; I've just got up."

"It doesn't bother me what you look like, Shiraz," said Murph. "I'm here to collect your kind donation."

"Donation?"

"Yes. Emily called me yesterday with her idea. I think it's absolutely brilliant. We've never done anything like it. It'll be something fresh and exciting, and I'm certain it will raise a lot of much-needed money."

"Come in. I'm sorry; I'm not sure what you're referring to."

We stepped down to the galley.

"Did Emily not tell you?" said Murph.

"She must've forgotten. What's going on?"

"Emily said you had loads of clothes to get rid of, and you were thinking of giving them to a charity shop. But she said some of them are really expensive, by posh designers. Me, I wouldn't be able to tell the difference between a designer dress and a ten pound one from Woolworth's, so they'd be lost on me."

"She's right. I do have several cases of clothes I'll probably never wear again."

"Sorry, Shiraz," said Emily's voice behind me. She stood in the bedroom door wearing a long T-shirt with her blonde bob in disarray. "I forgot to tell you, with all the excitement of yesterday evening."

"You two look like you've had a big night," said Murph. "It's a good job you're not on the boat today. So could I take the outfits? Are you okay with that? His eyes darted between Emily and me."

"I don't have any objection to donating them to Marine Rescue," I said to Murph. "Although I'm not sure what you plan to do with them. Here, let me show you." I opened the spare bedroom. "There are several cases, boxes and crates. Dresses, hats, shoes."

"Is this everything?" asked Murph.

"Yes. Are you sure you want them all?"

"Definitely."

Murph carried three suitcases at once, one under his arm and one in each hand. He then found he couldn't fit down the corridor to the steps up to the wheelhouse, and he was forced to carry them one by one. Emily and I passed hat boxes, shoe crates and bags up to him until the spare room was clear of them.

Murph returned downstairs. "Anything else?" he asked.

"Would you be interested in engine parts?" I said, pointing at the boxes left behind when I'd bought the barge. "How about a butterfly net?"

"I don't have any use for a butterfly net, but the engine parts might be of interest. He looked at the writing on the sides of the boxes. Ah, no. These are for diesel engines. The Marine Rescue boat runs on petrol. I'm not sure what you'll do with them. But these clothes will hopefully raise some money towards a new FLIR for the boat. Even though the handheld one saved a life on Friday, we can't count on it. It doesn't cover the area the roof mounted one does."

"I'm glad to have been able to help," I said.

"Right. Oh, and thank you so much for your proposal to host and star in the fashion parade."

"Fashion parade?" I frowned and turned to Emily.

She clenched her teeth. "I, um, may have omitted to tell you the exact details of your kind offer."

"Good luck," said Murph, winking at her. "I can't wait for this event. It'll be fantastic exposure for Redcliff Marine Rescue and raise money too."

Murph stomped up the steps, and I heard his van reverse away.

"Fashion parade?" I repeated to Emily. "Care to tell me what I've signed up for?"

She blushed. "You were a model, right?"

"Ye-es."

"And you know all about fashion?"

"I know something about fashion. Do go on."

"I may have suggested to Murph that you might like to model some of your old dresses, and we'll auction them at a fashion show." She stood in front of me and held both my arms. "Shiraz, you have to do this. I'll help you organise it. We need the new FLIR, and someone might lose their life if you don't agree."

"Woah. You're not emotional blackmailing me. Although I am aware Oscar's actions last night will have scuppered Lady Dulvington's donation."

"That's not all it scuppered," said Emily. "I think I'm starting to come to terms with what's happened, but I really liked Sean. It's like one of those things you read about in the papers, where someone's conned on a dating app by a person who reels them in with a promise of a relationship, and then they turn out to be a scammer."

"Oscar's such a wily old dog. He pretended to take an interest in Sean's supernatural theories and terminology. His change of stance on the paranormal aspect surprised me, but I should've known. He was a sceptic all along. And I suppose I am too, now. That image Sean showed us on the camera was just an out-of-focus shot he took earlier. And that ultraviolet umbrella; I don't think it did anything."

"But what about the wailing? And the figure in white?" asked Emily.

"You know what? I'm wondering if Sean somehow created them to perpetuate the myth and retain his payment? If not, maybe they were hares and barn owls? Oscar was right all along."

"I'm still not speaking to him," said Emily. "I will after a few days. But right now, I feel like my soul's been torn out of my body, and it's his fault."

"You can't blame Oscar," I said. "He wasn't to know how fond you were of Sean, and, besides, he would've had your best interests at heart. I need to cheer you up. Here's what we'll do. How about we go for a long walk, followed by dinner at the Smuggler's Tavern and a couple of Champagnes? My treat. We can discuss your fashion show Murph thinks I'm putting on. But that doesn't mean I've agreed to do it. Yet. I'll think about it."

"Really?" said Emily. She hugged me. "Thank you so much, Shiraz. I knew you'd come round to my idea. Oh. I hope I feel like eating by this evening. What do people call it? Lovesick?"

Despite Emily's misgivings, her appetite picked up as we walked all the way from Redcliff Harbour to East Beach and Golden Bay. Spring showers were interspersed with sunny spells, and we strolled, laughed and chatted, and tried to forget all about ghosts, entities, ley lines, paranormal investigators and anomalous phenomena.

I was quite taken by her fashion show idea, although I wasn't going to reveal that fact to her immediately. We compared notes on marine rescue and how much studying remained before becoming qualified crew. By the time we reached the Smuggler's Tavern, we were hungry enough to order a main course and a side salad each, and we polished off a bottle of Champagne.

"I have to open the café in the morning," said Emily, once we'd shared a dessert. "This has been a lovely afternoon and evening, but it's a quarter to nine, and we should start heading home. And thank you. You're a very very good friend, and I'm so happy you dropped anchor a few minutes away from my home."

"My pleasure. I know what a broken heart feels like. I'm here for you. Are you okay to walk?"

"I'm fine. I only drank two glasses."

We strolled along Redcliff seafront. The temperature had dropped, and a brisk evening breeze picked up.

"Stop," said Emily. "I can see Oscar and Cadbury in the distance, and I don't want to bump into them. It'll be awkward."

"Too late," I said. "He's waving. We'll say a quick 'hello'."

Cadbury tugged Oscar towards us and licked our hands.

"Good evening, ladies," said Oscar. "I've just come from your place, Shiraz, but you weren't home. I have news for you."

"Oh?" I said. "We've enjoyed a girly evening out. And I've got big news for you too. We're putting on a fashion show to raise money for Marine Rescue. I'll give you the details when I have them."

Emily clenched her fists and grinned. "So you'll do it? Definitely? Yes! That's so exciting."

"I will," I said. "But your punishment for putting me on the spot is that you have to model some of the clothes too."

"No way," said Emily. "I could never get up on a catwalk."

"We'll see," I said. "What was your news, Oscar?"

"I was coming to tell you we need to regroup immediately."

"Why? Sean's been exposed as a fraud, and the photo he showed us was fake. The noises probably were too."

"How do you explain this, then? I had a call today from Lady Dulvington. And she's reported hearing the noises again, and she clearly saw the ghost floating between the trees. Our investigation's a long way from over."

"This is ridiculous," I said, as we sat around my dining table and drank tea. Cadbury settled on the kitchen floor, hoping for a digestive biscuit. "We can't do another stakeout. We don't have Sean's equipment, although I suppose that was all useless, anyway."

"I agree," said Oscar. "I'm still ninety-five per cent sure animals or teenagers are causing these noises and sightings, and all the ghost-hunting equipment in the world won't help with them. But there's that five per cent that tells me Lady Dulvington's got all her faculties, and she's not fooling around. I think we're back to square one again with our investigation. And we did hear that strange noise ourselves, which we couldn't explain. An anomalous phenomenon."

"That was Sean's expression," said Emily.

"Sorry, was it? I must've picked it up from him."

Emily took a deep breath. "What led you to believe he was a fake?"

"I'd never met a ghost hunter before, so I wasn't sure how they were supposed to behave. And, you know me, I was suspicious. So I rang an old colleague in the police and asked if he'd ever heard of a case where someone had conned people by pretending to be a paranormal expert. He hadn't, but he searched on the computer and came up with this Jake Robinson chap. There was a warrant out for his arrest. Of course, he didn't tell me Jakes's name *per se*, but I described Sean to him, and we agreed they might've been the same person. So I told them where Sean would be, at what time, on what date and suggested the police might like to attend. Apparently, he's relieved over thirty gullible pensioners of their savings. And all from a small ad in *Country Lady* magazine."

"Part of me wishes you hadn't done that," said Emily, "and part of me's glad you did." She looked up at Oscar and smiled at him.

"So now what?" I asked.

"If we want to have any chance of earning the donation for Marine Rescue, we need to come up with some ideas. We'll have to organise another stakeout and try to witness the ghost ourselves."

"So, what, we just go up there one night and sit around on the off chance? We need to bring something with us to look like we know what we're doing."

"I agree," said Oscar. "I always carry my torch, but that's not enough."

"You could bring that butterfly net," suggested Emily to me. "If the ghost emerges, you could throw that over it and catch it."

"Is that the way ghosts work? I thought they passed through solid objects."

"Who knows? Take it anyway, as part of your ghost hunting kit."

"And I'll bring Cadbury," said Oscar. "He'll probably sleep through the whole affair, though. But even if Sean's suggestion about him being able to detect supernatural activity might've been rubbish, it's a fact that dogs have sharper hearing than humans. He might pick up the source of the strange noise."

I frowned and nodded, then smiled and clenched my fists.

Oscar and Emily turned to look at me.

"I've just had a great idea," I said. "If the ghost comes out to play, I know exactly how we could tell if it's really paranormal, or just someone cloaked in a sheet. But first, I need to borrow something from Murph."

CHAPTER TWENTY-ONE

"Hi, Murph. Could I ask you a favour?"

I walked towards the marine rescue vessel sitting on its trailer in the shed. Murph was leaning over its roof with a screwdriver in his hand.

"Morning, Shiraz. What brings you here today? I'm just taking the old FLIR apart to see if I can somehow fix it, but I've no hope without the right parts. We'll have to rely on the handheld one until we can replace it."

"Yes, the handheld one. I, err, was wondering if I could borrow it?"

"Pardon?"

"I was wondering if I could borrow the handheld FLIR. Just for tonight. I'll bring it back tomorrow morning."

"Electrifying echo sounders. Don't be ridiculous. What happens if we get a callout, and the main one lets us down again? We'll have nothing, and someone could drown."

"I know, I know. D'you think you'll be called out tonight?"

Murph glanced out of the door at storm clouds gusting across the sea. Shrubs along the seafront bent horizontally, and people clutched their coats around themselves.

"We've been paged in weather worse than this before. Why d'you want it?"

"Um, Emily and I plan to practice our night search patterns by walking around the recreation field at night, trying to find something. We want to be confident of getting signed off."

Murph's lips formed a straight line, and he puffed. "Sorry, Shiraz. Our equipment stays on the boat where it's needed." He returned to his screwdriver, and I stood beside the boat with my hands folded in front of me.

"What if I helped to buy a new FLIR for the boat?"

Murph stopped and stared at me. "D'you remember how much one costs? Twenty thousand pounds, including tax and fitting. I'm sure your fashion show will raise some of what's needed, but the residents of Redcliff won't have the money to pay full price for those dresses. We'll be lucky to finish up with half that sum."

I took a deep breath. "Murph, if you let me borrow the handheld FLIR tonight, I'll get a donation for the rest. Promise."

"You're serious, aren't you? Okay, I'll do you a deal, just because it's a stormy night, all the boats are in the harbour, and we're unlikely to get a call out. You can borrow the handheld FLIR for tonight only to practise searching. I'll lend you a pager, the same as the search and rescue crew carry. If the pager goes off, you must return here with the FLIR immediately. And this is all conditional on your offer to get the donation, however you plan to achieve that."

"That's wonderful, Murph; I promise I'll look after it."

"Sergeant Wainwright, thank you so much for returning." Lady Dulvington stood to greet us, and one of her Corgis flopped onto the floor. "You and your colleagues really have been a tower of strength to me throughout this entire business."

"I'm only glad we could be of assistance," said Oscar. "You need someone to rely on."

"Yes. Such a pity about the paranormal investigator. I was so taken in by him."

"As were many others, Lady Dulvington, as were many others. It transpires he has a history going back many years taking advantage of people in your position."

"He was so convincing. He showed me his credentials, which looked very professional and genuine."

"That's the reason he preys on older people," said Oscar. "A careful search of the World Wide Web confirmed that neither the University he claimed his degree from, nor the course he stated he was certified in, exist. But not everyone has access to the Internet, do they?"

"How silly of me. I should've asked Jennings to check. She's a whizz with computers, as all young people seem to be. D'you know, she was awarded High Distinction in her recent chemical engineering exam. She's so gifted."

We heard a sudden bang and the agitated voice of the butler. The door to the living room flew open, and in walked a short, skinny man dressed entirely in black. Barrowman tailed him, his mouth opening and closing without speaking.

"Can you give me five hundred pounds?" the man asked Lady Dulvington, while completely ignoring us. "I'll pay it back next week." Broken red veins covered his cheeks like a spider's web, and his bulbous nose appeared too large for his face. His grubby, misshapen T-shirt displayed food stains running down it, and his skinny jeans ended in a pair of worn, black cowboy boots.

Lady Dulvington stood. "Lucas, I wasn't expecting you today. Could I introduce Ms Shiraz Jones, Miss Emily..."

"Five hundred. That's all. It's not much to ask from someone of your riches, is it?"

"But, Lucas, I gave you five hundred last week. What are you doing with all this money?"

"That's my business. I just need another five. I'll take four hundred if you don't have enough."

Oscar stood. "Lucas, I was a police sergeant, and I've dealt with many people like you in my time. Your mother doesn't want to..."

Lucas took a step towards him. "I don't care if you're the King of England. This is between me and her." He jabbed a bony finger. "Keep out of our affairs."

Oscar raised his chin and stood between Lucas and Lady Dulvington, but she spoke first.

"Sergeant Wainwright, please leave this to me. Thank you for trying to help but, as Lucas says, this is a family matter." She reached into a handbag beside her and pulled out a cheque book. "Lucas, I haven't been to the bank since your visit last week. I'll have to give you a cheque." She turned to the first slip of paper and began to write.

"Quickly," said Lucas. He glanced at a mantelpiece clock. "I need the money now."

"Lucas," I said, leaning around Oscar to catch his eye. "While Lady Dulvington's writing, could I ask you a question?"

"Why?"

"Have you recently heard unexplained noises here at Alnchurch Park, or seen an apparition in white?"

I watched for a reaction, and noticed his complexion paled immediately.

"What are you talking about?" He turned to his mother. "Hurry up. Write faster."

"I'm talking about a ghost," I said.

Lady Dulvington turned to me and frowned, but her expression didn't indicate annoyance. More like anticipation.

"Ghost?" said Lucas.

The ceiling light reflected drops of sweat on his brow.

"Yes. A ghost. Here at the estate."

His eyes darted around the room. "There aren't any ghosts at the estate. Are there?"

"That's what I'm asking you, Lucas. Have you ever seen one?"

"I don't have time for this," he yelled. "I'm a busy man." He reached out his hand towards Lady Dulvington. "Give me the cheque," he shouted, and he snatched it from her, turned around and marched out, slamming the door behind him.

We froze and glanced at each other sideways. Lady Dulvington dipped her chin and covered her face with her hands.

Emily reached out for her. "Are you okay?" she asked.

Lady Dulvington sighed. "Yes. That, as you doubtless gathered, was my son. I'm not in the least bit proud of his actions. But he's right. I do have the means to provide for his needs, whatever they may be."

"What we just witnessed is correctly known as elder abuse," said Oscar. "Bordering on extortion. Would you allow me to ask the police at what point Lucas's actions become a criminal matter? I find it very hard to stand by and permit his behaviour to continue without taking some kind of action."

Lady Dulvington closed her eyes, sat up straight and opened them again. "Another time, Sergeant. Back to the matter in hand, please. Could we discuss tonight's plan?"

"Lady Dulvington," I said. "We may not have professional-looking equipment like a ghost hunter would have, but we're not going up to the ruins empty handed. We have a dog with us who may well be able to detect spirits appearing beyond the spectrum humans can see and hear."

Oscar wrinkled his lips, clenched his teeth and sucked in a breath.

I glanced sideways at him. "And if it really turns out to be hares, or foxes making the noise, he'll bark loudly."

"I hope he does," said Oscar under his breath.

I continued. "We have other equipment with us which will confirm the existence of a spirit. I know you have Sister Florrie and Sister Marie available to provide their opinions. If we see a real ghost and they do as well, there'll be no doubt this is a genuine supernatural haunting."

Lady Dulvington nodded. "I don't pretend to understand your equipment, just like I didn't understand the methods the man I knew as Mr Plumtree employed, but at least I trust you not to fool me. And if you're successful in getting to the bottom of this, I'll keep my promise to donate a significant sum to Marine Rescue."

"We won't let you down, Lady Dulvington," said Emily.

"Right," said Oscar. "Eight o'clock. Nearly dusk. We'll head up to the ruins and take up position for the evening. Rest assured, we will conclude this business, whatever the disturbances turn out to be."

Lady Dulvington allowed him to take her hand. "Thank you again, Sergeant," she said.

"You did a wonderful job of sounding confident," said Emily. "And the way you faced up to Lucas, I thought you two were about to have a fight."

"I wish I was as confident as I looked," said Oscar, untying Cadbury's lead from the post outside the gatehouse. "I met many people like Lucas in my life in the force. Cowards. Utter cowards. He's bullying an old lady who can't defend herself."

"She's her own worst enemy," I said. "If she stopped handing over money, he might leave her alone."

"Or the abuse might escalate. It makes my blood boil."

"D'you think Lucas is connected to the ghost?" asked Emily.

"I don't think so," I said. "I was very specific when asking him about it, and I watched his reaction carefully. You can't fake fear easily. Have you ever tried to deliberately make yourself sweat?"

"I've never even thought about it."

"Try it now. Go on."

"How? It's impossible."

"Exactly. And when I asked Lucas about the ghost, he sweated and trembled as if one stood in front of him. I think what Lady Dulvington told us about his experience with the circling footsteps in the lane outside is completely accurate. He's terrified of the thought of them."

"Goodness. I thought I was bad."

"Regardless, Lady Dulvington's counting on us," said Oscar. He addressed the dog. "Cadbury, you're our trump card tonight."

Cadbury looked at him quizzically.

"You, my canine friend, are going to bark loudly if you see a hare or a fox, or if you see a teenager dressed in a sheet. If you see a real ghost, I want you to howl. Got it?" Oscar laughed, while the dog continued to stand beside him, blissfully unaware of his multiple responsibilities.

"Should I fetch the butterfly net from the car?" I asked.

"Presumably that's the other equipment you told Lady Dulvington about?" said Emily. "I suppose we might catch an animal in it, or even a person. But wouldn't a ghost go right through the netting?"

"I don't know what a ghost will do, and we may never find out. But I have something else with me that will definitely help." I reached inside my coat pocket and showed the contents to her.

She gasped. "The portable FLIR. Don't tell me you pinched that from the rescue boat. Murph would absolutely skin you alive if he knew you'd got that."

"He knows, Emily. I asked him if I could borrow it. I'm counting on this little device to help with our hunt for ghosts much more than Sean's cameras did."

"Really?" said Oscar. "We didn't have one of those on the boat when I was a skipper. Why would Marine Rescue own a device to detect ghosts?"

"It won't detect ghosts. But it will detect body heat. And if the white phantom really is a teenager in a sheet, or it's caused by any kind of human activity, we'll know as soon as we point the FLIR at it."

Emily grinned. "Shiraz, you're a genius. But how on earth did you persuade Murph to lend you the portable FLIR? He never lets any equipment go walkies from the shed. And with the main one broken, he'll need it, won't he?"

"Yes, but if we solve the mystery, Lady Dulvington's donation will go a long way towards paying for a new roof-mounted FLIR. Murph's only condition was that I took a pager with me, so if the rescue boat's called out, I have to return the portable FLIR immediately."

"But we're in Alnchurch. It'll take twenty minutes for you to get back to Redcliff."

"I know. Oops."

"Shiraz Jones, you are trouble. With a capital 'T'. You'd better pray that pager stays silent all night."

"Come on," said Oscar. "Let's walk up there and get in position before it's pitch black."

We marched down the track and crossed the river at the little footbridge. Cadbury tugged at his lead as our approach frightened a rabbit enjoying a pre-bedtime snack.

"See?" I said. "He'll tell us if the noise really is a hare."

"I have my doubts," said Oscar. "He'll be asleep within ten minutes of us taking up position."

"Could you carry the butterfly net for a bit, Emily?" I asked. "It's awkward, and my hand's getting cramp."

"Okay. Goodness knows what we're going to do with this. I'm very nervous without Sean here. Even if he was a fake, his expert knowledge felt very reassuring. And helping him with his equipment took my mind off the spookiness."

I rubbed her shoulder and passed her the net as we left the main track and walked up through the trees. A full moon shone behind clouds scudding across the blackening sky.

It was a perfect night for a haunting.

We took up our position seated on the low walls. Oscar gripped Cadbury's lead, Emily held the butterfly net like a shepherd's staff, and I switched the FLIR on to test it. I shone it at Emily, and she showed up as a white blob.

"Ready?" I said. "Nine o'clock. Witching hour."

Time passed, and I shuffled my bottom. Cadbury stood and shook himself, which caused brief excitement, then turned around and flopped again at Oscar's feet.

Emily laid the net down and sighed. "It's not going to come tonight, is it? Another evening wasted. And I have to open the café tomorrow, exhausted again."

"Shh," I said. "The noises have been heard several times, and Lady Dulvington said most nights the phantom in white's appeared too. Wait."

We waited.

The trees rustled in the breeze.

A distant owl hooted.

Cadbury breathed out loudly and lay down with all four legs stretched out.

Suddenly, several things happened at once.

"Shiraz, the noise is starting." Emily gripped my arm and shuffled closer to me as the same wailing we'd heard earlier echoed around us.

Cadbury sat up and put his head on one side.

Oscar stood and gazed around. "It sounds the same as the other night. Filling the air. Directionless. Impossible to tell where it's coming from. Cadbury, what do you think?"

Encouraged by his master's actions, Cadbury stood like the gun dog he was, ready to retrieve whatever might fall from the skies.

He didn't have long to wait.

Emily screamed as an apparition in white floated towards us.

"Shiraz, that's not a human," she whimpered. "Humans don't float."

"Wait. Let me switch on the FLIR." I clicked the button, and the screen lit up. I pointed it at the floating object, which seemed to be a head with a white robe hanging from it, exactly like a cartoon image of a ghost.

The FLIR's screen remained blank.

"It's not giving off a heat signature, Shiraz," said Emily, gripping my arm harder. "It's an actual ghost." She covered her eyes with her hand and peeked between her fingers.

The phantom rose and fell a few feet above the ruins, never touching them. It glided from the ballroom across the hall where we sat and flew into the dining room. My scalp prickled, and if I'd had a mirror handy, I wouldn't have been surprised to see my hair standing on end. The omnipresent humming continued.

We watched the apparition circumnavigate the dining room, then it performed a sudden turn and came back towards us. Emily screamed again, and Cadbury tugged Oscar's arm and barked as it approached.

"Good dog," said Oscar. "Scare it off."

The dog strained at his lead, continually woofing at the floating white apparition. I aimed the FLIR directly at the phantom, but the screen continued to show the same blank view as if I'd been aiming it at an empty patch of sea. No heat signature.

The ghost floated from side to side, then dramatically swerved in our direction. Its face had no features, which made it even more terrifying.

"It's coming for us," yelled Emily. "Help!" She ducked behind me and gripped me with both arms.

Cadbury's deep bark echoed around the area.

I aimed the FLIR as if I was a priest holding a holy cross at a demon.

The phantom swooped lower so that it almost touched the ground. Cadbury exploded in barks.

"The butterfly net," I hissed to Emily. "When it dives again, catch it."

"You catch it," she said. "I can't move. My legs won't work." She trembled behind me.

I stuffed the FLIR in my pocket and lifted the handle of the net slowly. The ghost probably didn't care about my actions, but I felt like it shouldn't know what I was doing.

Suddenly, Cadbury yanked his lead out of Oscar's grip and, as if in slow motion, the Labrador sprinted towards the ghost, leapt several feet in the air and gripped the bottom of it in his teeth.

I swiped the butterfly net, and we watched in horror as the ghost's dangling sheet enveloped Cadbury, and he vanished under it.

CHAPTER TWENTY-TWO

The ghost crashed to the ground with the net on top of it and Cadbury underneath. Oscar rushed towards them. He leapt on the sheet in a rugby tackle and, simultaneously, the humming noise ceased. Cadbury continued to bark as Oscar untangled him.

I dropped the handle of the net and breathed heavily. Emily collapsed onto one of the low walls and panted.

We stared at Oscar, torch in one hand, standing over the ghost. Cadbury sat at his feet and grinned, his tongue lolling to one side.

"What is it?" I asked.

Oscar held up a white sheet and a ball. "It's a white cloth with some kind of sphere inside it. Let's have a better look at our so-called ghost."

Oscar directed the beam of his torch, and we sat on the walls at the corner of the hall to inspect the object Cadbury had caught. Emily repeatedly glanced up as if she expected more phenomena to appear, but Oscar was convinced we'd solved the entire mystery. The ghost comprised a lightweight black sphere slightly smaller than a football, and a white piece of cloth glued to it, which had probably once been part of a bedsheet.

Oscar tore the sheet from the ball with a ripping noise and held up the sphere. A small hole had been drilled in one end.

"How did it fly by itself?" asked Emily. She stepped back from it, as if the thing was about to come to life in Oscar's hands.

He held it up to his ear and shook it. We heard rattling; the same noise you'd hear from a broken toy like a kaleidoscope.

"Can anyone find a stone?" asked Oscar, shining his torch around the ground.

"Here's one," I said, and I passed him a small lump of rock which was once part of the walls of the house.

He took it, placed the sphere on the ground and gave it a sharp tap. It cracked, and a hole appeared in it.

"Papier mâché," said Oscar. He handed me the torch, placed the fingers of both hands in the hole and pulled them apart. The gap became larger, and he turned the sphere upside down and shook it. Metal and plastic parts fell onto the ground with nuts and bolts which looked like they came from a Meccano set. One heavier item remained inside and wouldn't come out through the hole. I shone the torch in, and we read the initials 'DJI' stamped on it.

"It's a drone," said Oscar. "DJI manufacturers parts for drones. My son's company supplies cases for them."

"But how did it fly?" I asked. "When I attended Marc Anthony and Nadia Ferreira's wedding in Miami last year, I remember paparazzi bothering us with drones, and they all had rotor blades like helicopters. I don't see how a sphere would fly."

"See this hole in the top," said Oscar. "If we hunt around where it crashed, I reckon we'll find a rod and some blades." He took the torch and inspected the ground.

Cadbury followed him in case he was required for any more supernatural entrapments.

"Here," said Oscar. He held up parts similar to those we'd found when we combed through the ruins the previous week. "That's all the ghost was. A cleverly adapted drone."

"Is that it?" said Emily. "Have we finished our assignment? Can we collect our reward so Murph can use it?"

"Not yet," I said. "Because where there's a drone, there'll be a drone operator nearby."

"But how will we find them in the dark?"

I brandished the handheld FLIR. "Easy. Follow me. It's time to practice a sector search."

We combed the ruins in our Trivial-Pursuit-counter pattern, pointing the FLIR at every shrub and up every tree. At one point, I thought I'd found the culprit, but the device had detected the body heat of a badger in its burrow under a gigantic oak tree.

"What's the range of a drone?" asked Emily.

"It could be over a mile, but I suspect the operator's not that far away. They'd have had to see the drone all the time, because it didn't have a camera, and someone was steering it fairly precisely. They're watching from close by."

"That gives me the creeps as much as the ghost did," said Emily.

We hunted along the perimeter walls of the ruined house. Many of them were nothing more than an outline on the ground, but some, such as the ones we'd been sitting on, were high enough for a person to have hidden behind them. But the FLIR screen remained blank.

We searched towards the rear of the entrance hall, where the original stairway would have been.

Near the back of the room, by the thick wall, the FLIR picked up a faint signal.

"Emily, Oscar. There's something in this wall. The FLIR's showing it to be warmer than the surrounding stones."

The two of them peered around me at the screen.

"Are you sure that's not a false reading?" asked Oscar. "Maybe the sun was shining on that stone during the day, and it still retains some heat."

"No. None of the other walls nearby give the same heat signature." I thumped the wall with my fist, but it felt the same as any other stone. I stood back and gazed at the wall, the most complete one remaining in the entire ruin. Deep cracks between the stones showed where they joined, and the mortar had disintegrated. I stood right at the foot of the wall to reach up and feel it and, as I did, my foot sank into the ground.

"Oscar. Over here, with your torch."

He pointed the torch at the base of the wall, and I knelt and scooped away clumps of dry grass. A depression appeared, and my excavations continued until we discovered a very low hole directly under the wall.

I pointed the FLIR into the hole, and it lit up two white, vertical blobs, which I concluded were the bottom of someone's legs.

"Come out," I said. "We know you're in there."

"Who is it?" whispered Emily. She hid behind me.

"I can't tell yet. Wait."

A pair of stout shoes emerged, soles first. Then a pair of legs. The person slithered out on their front, and their head was the last part of them to emerge.

The person sat up. Mud and leaves caked their hair, and they held a remote control in their left hand.

Emily covered her mouth. "It's Jennings," she said.

"Jennings?" I asked. "What's going on?"

Jennings put down the remote, looked up at me, bit her lip and swallowed.

"What are you doing, Jennings?" I asked. "What's all this about?"

Oscar stared at her sternly. "I've no idea what you're up to, but you're in big trouble. We'll go straight down to the gatehouse to tell Lady Dulvington. She'll be very surprised to discover the real reason for the so-called paranormal activity."

Jennings sighed. "She won't be surprised in the slightest. It was her idea."

CHAPTER TWENTY-THREE

"Sir?" said Barrowman, peeking his nose around the front door of the gatehouse. The time was after 10:00 p.m., and I had felt our chances of anyone answering our knock would be minimal.

"I'm aware it's late, Barrowman," said Oscar, "but it's imperative we speak with Lady Dulvington immediately." He tied Cadbury's lead to the post outside.

"Her ladyship will be retiring shortly, sir. I have this moment taken her an evening cup of Ovaltine."

"She's still awake, then? Good. Please advise her that Sergeant Wainwright is calling, together with his associates and Miss Jennings, and we wish to speak with her right away."

"Very good, sir. Please wait here."

He closed the front door, and we stood in the porch light's glow.

"Why won't you tell us what this is about?" Oscar asked Jennings. "Why disturb Lady Dulvington at this time of night?"

"I'm not telling you anything. It's not my place," said Jennings. "You need to hear it from her."

Barrowman opened the door. "Her ladyship will see you now. This way."

We followed him into the living room. Lady Dulvington sat in her usual chair with a hot drink and a glass of dark-red Port wine. The three Corgis slept around her in various positions, one on its back with its legs akimbo which brought a smile to my lips. She wore a full-length satin dressing gown, accompanied by a shawl around her shoulders, and a blanket lay across her knees. I idly thought how elegant she looked, and I hoped I looked as good when I was almost ninety.

Jennings strode over to her, sat on the edge of her chair and draped her arm around the old lady's shoulders. "They know," she said. "I'm so sorry. I've failed you."

Lady Dulvington sighed. "You haven't failed me, Zoe. You could never fail me."

Oscar stood with his fists on his hips. "We discovered Miss Jennings hiding in the ruins. It seems she constructed…"

Lady Dulvington held up one hand, and Oscar paused. "Please, sit down," she said. "Even though it's late, it's time for us all to hear a bedtime story." She fluffed the blanket around her legs. "Are you sitting comfortably? Then I'll begin."

We sat quietly in the same seats we'd occupied when we visited before. I folded my hands in my lap and studied Lady Dulvington expectantly.

She closed her eyes, and for a moment I thought she'd drifted off to sleep. Then she shook her head and opened them.

"Where were we up to? When you visited me last time, I told you the story about my invalid father, and how he'd made his nurse pregnant, much to my grandfather's chagrin."

"Yes," I said. "You mentioned your grandfather's housekeeper brought you up, on the pretence that the baby was her late sister's."

"Ah, yes. Permit me to continue. My grandfather explained my presence by saying the housekeeper's sister had died in childbirth, and there was no one else to bring me up. My father passed away from his illness shortly afterwards and, although my grandfather had originally planned to have nothing to do with me, he realised I was the only descendant of the family, the only one who could continue the Dulvington line, and his closest blood relative. So he spent more and more time with me and, as I grew up and became more independent, his love for me, and mine for him, grew. Eventually, everybody accepted I was his granddaughter, and the circumstances of my birth were glossed over. I'm sure some ill-meaning villagers engaged in idle tittle-tattle, but people respected my grandfather, and certainly nothing was said in public."

Lady Dulvington took a sip of the port in the little glass, and dabbed her lips with a small, white handkerchief. We waited expectantly for her story to continue.

"In those days," she said, "when I was a child, Alnchurch Park was fully self-sufficient. We had our own cows for dairy products, horses, chickens, geese, pigs, and we even ground our own corn with the windmill to make bread."

She smiled with her eyes closed, and I watched the years fall off her expression as she relived her childhood.

"Then the Nazis came." Her face clouded over. "We hoped we'd be spared out here in the countryside, but weaponry was inaccurate in those days and, in the middle of the night, we took a direct hit. Fortunately, the bomb missed the main bedrooms where my grandfather and I were sleeping, but the roof fell in, and the staircase was destroyed. Fire engines from Redcliff, Alnchurch and even Headland Bay attended, and a firefighter carried me out of my bedroom window and down a ladder. The staff, together with the fire brigade, extinguished the flames, but the house was severely damaged. We retreated to live in the remaining habitable rooms, but they became less and less safe and, by the 1950s, the house was completely condemned."

"And the housekeeper, your adoptive mother, died?" asked Oscar.

"Yes. She perished, and I wasn't sorry. To my shame, I convinced myself that God had sent the bomb to rid me of her. My grandfather doted on me, and I spent the next ten years running wild with barely any supervision."

"Did he ever think of rebuilding?" asked Emily.

"Naturally," said Lady Dulvington. "Although it would have meant almost starting from scratch. Only one wall remained undamaged above head height, the one behind the grand staircase. It was, ironically, the oldest wall in the house, dating back to the time of Queen Elizabeth I. But the funds required would've been astronomical, and we would've been forced to sell much of our land to pay for it, which he was reluctant to do. He consulted a builder, but in the post-war years, materials for reconstructing such a large residence weren't available. Then my grandfather passed away after a short illness, and I inherited Alnchurch Park: the house, the grounds, the windmill; everything. By that stage, the house could no longer be inhabited. So I retreated to the gatehouse, and here I am still. And Alnchurch Park has never been rebuilt and never will be."

Oscar leant forward and clasped his hands together. "This is a fascinating story, Lady Dulvington. But it doesn't explain tonight's events."

"Sergeant Wainwright, I commend your urgency. But the story's completeness is important for your understanding, so may I ask you to have patience?"

One of the Corgis rolled over and grunted. Lady Dulvington glanced up at Jennings and smiled. "Losing my grandfather created a vast chasm in my life. In a bid to plug it, after a short period of mourning, I married too quickly for my own good. I wed a man from Scotland by the name of Giles Barr, who appeared to be a well-to-do businessman. I convinced myself that he could provide the money to rebuild and negate the need to sell any of the grounds."

She sighed. "The reality was quite the opposite. Giles saw me as his provider, and he contributed little. He was a lover of expensive whiskies and rarely consumed less than a bottle each evening. And when he drank, he turned into an unpleasant, violent and threatening person. It became obvious that he was not a man with whom I wanted to share my life, or even my house. Despite our unsteady relationship, I gave birth to a son, who we named Lucas. And not long after Lucas's birth, my husband's whisky habit claimed his life."

"He died of a heart condition, or liver disease?" I asked.

"He never made it as far as that," said Lady Dulvington. "One evening, after he'd consumed his regulation bottle of whisky, he stepped outside for a cigarette. I wouldn't let him smoke inside because of the baby. Suddenly, he raced back in, calling for the antique pistol he kept on the mantelpiece. I asked him what on earth he wanted that for at ten o'clock in the evening. Plus, he'd had so much to drink, I couldn't see how he'd be able to shoot straight. He told me he'd heard footsteps in the lane outside, a scrunch-scrunch-scrunching sound going around in a circle, and he was going to scare off the intruders."

Lady Dulvington clenched one fist. "I pleaded with him to reconsider. I told him, it was probably just a local resident coming home late at night; in those days, our lane was the chief route between Redcliff and Alnchurch. He said the footsteps kept walking around and around the lane, but he couldn't see anyone. He stormed out, and I ran after him, but I paused at the front door. I heard him yell in his strong Scottish accent, 'Show yourself, you coward.' Then I jumped at the sound of an explosion, followed by silence."

Lady Dulvington held her breath, then exhaled. "I called out, 'Giles!' but there was no answer. My eyes peered into the gloom, and I walked gingerly towards the gate. I didn't want him to shoot me, thinking I was the intruder."

"Very sensible," said Oscar. "If anyone keeps a gun in their house, the most likely person they'll shoot is themselves."

"And that's exactly what had happened, Sergeant Wainwright. In his drunken state, and in the dark, he'd held the gun the wrong way around and blown the side of his own head off. I ran out to find him lying in the driveway, dead as a doornail."

"I'm so sorry," said Emily.

"Don't be," said Lady Dulvington. "His death was a relief, a weight off my mind. But it left me alone with my son, Lucas. I had Barrowman, of course, but he had no experience in childcare. So I employed a woman to help me bring him up, a nanny, I suppose you'd have called her. The years passed, and Lucas grew up, sadly, inheriting the traits of the father he never knew. From the age of thirteen, he would strike me if we had a disagreement and, at fifteen years old, he began on the path of drink which had led to his father's ruin. I couldn't control him, but he'd listen to his nanny, and she was the only one who had any influence over him. She couldn't prevent him drinking, but he would curb his violence when she was around, and for that reason, I retained her in my employment until he was in his late teens."

"But you don't employ her now?" I asked.

"She hasn't worked for me for many years," said Lady Dulvington. "But her daughter did for a while."

Lady Dulvington glanced at Oscar, who was checking his watch.

"Bear with me, Sergeant," she said. "This will all make perfect sense soon, and you'll understand how my story connects with tonight's events. Once Lucas became a young man, his nanny didn't want to work for me anymore. She explained there wasn't really anything for her to do now Lucas had grown up, and she enjoyed working with young children. She'd accepted a post in Redcliff, working for a couple with two small girls. I accepted her resignation with some regret, and asked if she knew anyone who could assist me with daily duties around the house, which was a task she'd performed for me in her spare time. She told me her daughter was looking for part-time work, and she'd ask her. When I met the daughter, she seemed perfect. Around twenty-one years old, she worked in a hospice in the evenings and wanted some extra employment. So I took her on for three mornings per week, and she performed her duties very well. But then…" Lady Dulvington covered her eyes and stared at the floor.

She lifted her head, and Jennings rubbed her back.

"Then, Lucas and the daughter began a relationship. I did everything I could to dissuade it, as I imagined the poor girl would suffer at his hands, as I had at his father's. I'd seen his violent streak and suffered it myself. But the young lady thought she could change him. She believed she could cure him of his issues. She couldn't, and within three months of her starting work, she'd resigned from my employment."

"Did he harm her?"

"Probably. I didn't see it first hand, but I caught her weeping. Poor, poor girl. I felt responsible because I was the one who'd introduced them."

"It wasn't your fault," said Emily. "You could never have imagined they'd be attracted to each other."

"No. I suppose not. Anyway, after she left, I employed another woman to help, and deliberately selected a person from a much older generation, so the same wouldn't happen again."

"There's a lot to be said for mature employees," said Oscar. "Can we discuss tonight's events now?"

"Patience, Sergeant Wainwright. We can't turn to the end of a book to discover who committed the crime without reading all the chapters, can we? Anyway, around six months later,

Barrowman entered and told me there was a woman at the door to see me; the girl who used to work for me, the one who Lucas had taken a fancy to. I imagined she was looking for an employer's reference, perhaps, so I asked him to show her in. She entered, clothed in a long, white, flowing summer dress. I can picture the scene in my mind now. I offered her tea, and asked how I could help her. She stood in front of me, smoothed the dress against her belly and said, 'It's Lucas's.'"

"What was Lucas's?" asked Emily.

"Her baby. She was seven months pregnant with Lucas's child. My grandchild, biologically."

"Gosh," I said. "The same situation over again. Your father with his nurse, and your son with your daily help."

"Quite right, Ms Jones. It was the writer Mark Twain who said, 'History doesn't repeat itself, but it often rhymes'. And this piece of history was rhyming more than a children's picture book."

"What did you do next?" asked Emily.

"What could I do? This wasn't like the period between the wars when I was born. I knew the pain of losing my birth mother; the primal wound, they call it."

I smiled at her and reached out as if to touch her lightly. The primal wound was all too familiar to me too.

Lady Dulvington continued. "Things were different in the late 1990s. Illegitimate babies didn't have to be hidden away or brought up in the pretence of being someone else's. But I knew that if I told Lucas he was a father, he could've reacted badly. I didn't want him to find out, for the safety of the girl and the baby she was about to have. I asked her if she wanted Lucas to know, and to my relief, she said she didn't. She said she wasn't a gold digger, but because she wouldn't be able to work anymore once the child was born, she asked if I could see my way to helping her out financially. Of course I agreed; the sum she was asking for was trivial, and this baby was my flesh and blood. We both decided that Lucas would never know about his child, for its own safety, and the safety of its mother."

"That was a big secret for you to live with," said Emily. "Did you ever see the girl again, or did she just take your money and run?"

"I visited her every week, until her death two years ago from leukaemia, poor woman. Thankfully, the end was quick, and she didn't suffer for months on end like so many cancer patients. But, until that point, I saw her each week and provided enough money to ensure her and the child's needs were met."

"And Lucas never knew about this arrangement?"

"He never did, and he still doesn't."

"And the child?" I asked. "What became of him?"

Lady Dulvington clasped her hands together and squeezed her moist eyes closed. The words caught in her throat, and she struggled to speak.

Zoe Jennings pushed herself off the arm of the couch and stood. She met eyes with the three of us, then said, "The child wasn't a him. It was a her."

CHAPTER TWENTY-FOUR

Lady Dulvington looked up at Jennings, gave her a watery smile, and her hand reached out. "You're all I have now," she said.

I stared at Jennings, then at Lady Dulvington. And I noticed resemblances. The set of the jaw, the colour of the eyes, the shape of the ears. If Lady Dulvington had red hair, the similarity would've been even greater.

"Zoe Jennings is your granddaughter?"

"She is," said Lady Dulvington. "My precious, precious girl."

"Who else knows this?" asked Oscar.

Lady Dulvington blew out her cheeks. "Only Barrowman. No one else, now Zoe's mother's gone. And he wouldn't tell a soul. He's a very loyal, discreet man, as a butler should be. I've often asked Zoe whether she'd like to meet her birth father, to have a relationship with him, but it's never interested her."

"Why would I want to meet a man with an alcohol problem and a history of violence?" asked Zoe, rhetorically. "Granny's my family." She sat back on the Chesterfield's arm.

"Once Zoe's mother died," said Lady Dulvington, "employing her as my daily help was the best way for us to see each other regularly, without our relationship being exposed."

Zoe smiled conspiratorially. "We had to be very careful no one suspected our reading evenings, didn't we, Granny?"

"Indeed, my dear. And now, it's well past my bedtime. I must ask Barrowman to see you out."

"The ghost?" spluttered Oscar. "The fake ghost, with Jennings at the controls? I apologise, Lady Dulvington, but you engaged us to investigate a haunting at Alnchurch Park, and we've discovered what I suspected all along. There is no ghost. The noises and apparitions were made by natural means, namely Zoe Jennings, who we now know to be your granddaughter. Your story doesn't end here."

Lady Dulvington clasped her hands together and leant on them. "No, indeed. It is me who should apologise, Sergeant Wainwright. You're right. I, or we, owe you an explanation."

She sighed. "My wish was for Zoe to inherit the estate after my death. She objected, stating that local gossips would see her, a servant, as depriving the man no one knew was her biological father of his natural birthright. But how could I leave this life knowing that the estate was in the hands of someone who'd probably sell it to the first developer and waste the proceeds on drink? No, I was determined I'd leave Alnchurch Park to Zoe. But when I visited my lawyers to update my will, a family firm which my father and my grandfather both trusted, they informed me I couldn't disinherit Lucas as easily as I'd hoped. The estate comes with a conditional clause which my great-great-grandfather created. He was nearly cut out of his own father's will, and he didn't want history to repeat, or rhyme, to quote Mark Twain again. His fear was that Alnchurch Park would be left to somebody who didn't appreciate the family history, a more distant relative who had no personal connection to the estate. So he made a perpetual decree, and the lawyers believe it to be irreversible. Alnchurch Park, its grounds and the house could only be inherited by the eldest male heir. The sole exception is if there is no male heir, or if the eldest male heir declines the bequest. So I inherited the house and grounds together with the title, because I was my father's only child, he predeceased my grandfather, and I had no brothers."

"And the lawyer said you must leave it to Lucas as the eldest, in fact the only, male heir?" I asked.

"Yes. But I told Zoe I could never do that. It was my wish for her to inherit the estate, however undeserving she felt." Lady Dulvington turned to Zoe. "In my eyes, you deserve it more than anyone. You're the only one who would appreciate the family history I've taught you over the time we've had together."

"I see the dilemma," said Oscar. "When your great-great-grandfather made that ruling, he didn't anticipate that a Dulvington eldest son would be unsuitable to inherit. He imagined they'd all be like him, invested in the lineage of the Dulvington family and with the estate's best interests at heart."

"Exactly. Eventually, Zoe came around to my way of thinking, and we put our heads together to consider the two exceptions to my ancestor's ruling. The first is if no male heir exists, which obviously they do. Lucas is alive, if not entirely in his right mind. And we weren't about to murder him, although metaphorically the thought has crossed my mind many times. The second exception is if the male heir declines the bequest."

"That was the catalyst for our plan," said Zoe. "We had to make Alnchurch Park unattractive to Lucas, somewhere that he feared, and he wouldn't care if he inherited or not."

Lady Dulverton's eyes gleamed as she related her scheme, and her earlier tiredness evaporated. "I asked myself, 'What does Lucas want?' and the answer was easy: Money. Money to fund his errant lifestyle. And then I asked myself, 'What would make Lucas decline the bequest? What would make him say to Zoe after I'd gone, 'Take it. I don't want it.' And the answer was, if it was proved to be haunted. Imagine if you'd seen a horror movie which had scared you half to death, and then you inherited the haunted house in the film? You wouldn't want to go within a mile of the place. Lucas was terrified of ghosts. Petrified. But I wasn't convinced the one experience he'd had as a boy in the lane outside was sufficient. I needed to make him believe the house was haunted by malicious spirits, just like a movie house of horrors. And how would I do that?"

Oscar folded his arms and sighed. "I suppose you came up with this madcap scheme to use Jennings' engineering experience to build a mechanical ghost, and then make sure reliable witnesses, such as me and a so-called professional paranormal investigator, witnessed it."

"Exactly." Lady Dulvington clapped her hands three times. "I was so impressed when Zoe showed me her creation. She told me she'd made it as part of an assessment at university, and she'd received a high distinction."

Zoe grinned. "I adapted a drone with a papier mâché surround and configured it to fly. I had several attempts, and more than one drone crash landed up at the ruins. Eventually, I designed one that would float in the air, without it being obvious it was a drone. I covered it with the thinnest, lightest sheet I could find and *voila*! One ghost."

Oscar flicked his gaze upward and minutely shook his head.

"What about the spooky sound?" asked Emily. "How did you create that? It was terrifying, like nothing I've heard before."

"Software engineering is part of my course," said Zoe. "I built an app which would create the noise. Then I coded it so I could control it remotely. I left a mobile phone paired to a powerful portable speaker inside the hole where you found me hiding, and I could start or stop the noise from my phone wherever I was. It echoed around splendidly, don't you think? I received a high distinction for that piece of work too."

"I'm so proud of your achievements," said Lady Dulvington. "You're a true Dulvington. I wish my grandfather were alive to meet you."

"I've been completely taken for a fool," said Oscar. "Although I knew this wasn't anything supernatural. I considered it might be animals, such as hares, but all the time it was you and your engineering skills."

I rubbed my chin. "That hole in the wall where you kept the speaker, and where we found you with the drone remote control. How did you know it was there? It was right inside the thick walls, in the part of the house which dates back to the 1500s."

"It was a priest hole," said Lady Dulvington.

"What's a priest hole?"

"Elizabeth I, bless her, took great exception to the Catholic church, and enacted several measures against priests, including torture and execution. She engaged priest hunters, people who specifically sought out priests and brought them to court to be tried and hanged. After 1570, hiding holes were built into houses to secrete priests from these bounty hunters and, as you've discovered tonight, they were nearly impossible to find."

Zoe grinned. "This one benefited from a crack through which I could see where to fly the ghost. Ingenious, don't you think?"

Oscar drummed his fingers. "So now what d'you want us to do, Lady Dulvington? We know Alnchurch Park isn't really haunted, so we can't testify we've seen spirits here. Nor can the ghost hunter, as he turned out to be a fraud himself. We're no use at all to your inheritance scheme."

"Sergeant Wainwright, on the contrary. Your presence here has enabled me to put part two of my plan into practice."

CHAPTER TWENTY-FIVE

"Part two of your plan?" asked Oscar. "What's part two? Will Zoe build some kind of dancing robotic skeleton?"

"Nothing so dramatic, Sergeant. Part two of my plan is as follows." Lady Dulvington looked at each of us. "Knowing what you've heard from me this evening, could any of you bring yourselves to tell anyone else what you discovered tonight? Look inside yourselves. Would you stand up and make a statement, in the sure knowledge you'd hand Alnchurch Park to a violent drunk, rather than an intelligent young lady who'll look after the estate in the way I and my grandfather would've wanted?"

Oscar shook his head and uncrossed his legs. "Lady Dulvington, I'm an ex-police officer and the acting mayor of Redcliff. I can't simply lie about what I've witnessed."

"You don't have to lie, Sergeant. None of you do. With a clear conscience, I can state hand on heart that the respected police sergeant Oscar Wainwright and his two associates from emergency services have investigated the presence of a ghost here, and they've witnessed events they weren't expecting. They've seen things which have alarmed them and heard sounds which they've described as terrifying. Is any of that sentence false, Sergeant?"

Oscar puffed loudly. "Not strictly, no."

"Good. All of this activity should be enough to put Lucas off ever demanding his birthright. On top of that, I'll make sure he receives a suitable sum of money to allow him to rehabilitate. I won't completely cast him aside, despite our troubled relationship."

Oscar folded his arms and gazed at the ceiling. One of the Corgis woke up, stood and looked at him with its tongue out, as if it suspected him of secreting a pork sausage in his pocket.

I tapped my fingers together. "Lady Dulvington, on the subject of sums of money, could I confirm our engagement is now complete, and you'll be transferring your donation to Redcliff Marine Rescue?"

"Naturally, Ms Jones. How would you like the funds?"

"The bank details for donations are on our website."

"Excellent. Zoe can find them for me. I'll transfer ten thousand pounds tomorrow. Thank you so much for coming, Sergeant. Ms Jones, Miss Philpot, your input has been invaluable. Goodness, it's very late. Almost midnight. The witching hour, one might say."

Oscar sighed and stood. He held Lady Dulvington's hand. "I'm still not sure where I stand on all this, but I suppose I'm glad to have been of service."

The butler showed us out to the driveway where we found Cadbury waiting for us, wagging his tail.

"Hello, boy," said Oscar, unclipping his lead. "Can you keep a secret? If anyone asks, just tell them you attacked an alarming, mysterious, white, floating object. None of that sentence is false, is it, Cadbury?" He ruffled the dog's head, and we piled into Emily's car.

CHAPTER TWENTY-SIX

One week later

Emily, Oscar and I sat in the Smuggler's Tavern sharing a bottle of sparkling wine. The weather was warming up, and I felt comfortable enough to wear a sleeveless top.

"Is everyone ready for tonight's fashion show?" asked Emily. "Our target's ten thousand pounds. Murph was over the moon with Lady Dulvington's donation, but he reminded me it was only half of what we need for the new FLIR."

"I'm ready," I said. "I don't need any practice at quick dress changes. And thank you so much for agreeing to compere the show, Oscar. I always thought Murph would do it, but he said he's not comfortable speaking in front of so many people, especially on an unfamiliar subject."

"It'll be a significantly pleasanter task than helping Lady Dulvington with her little inheritance scheme, regardless of how much she donated," said Oscar. "I feel like she's completely played me. Lady Dulvington's a very clever woman. She knows exactly how to get her own way, without it looking as if that was her intention. Honestly, I prefer investigating murders. At least you know where you stand with a dead body."

"The entire experience has been an extraordinary ride," said Emily. "When we started on this journey, I was terrified of ghosts. Then I met Sean, and his almost scientific knowledge of them made me think of ghosts as being something you study, like birds. On that devastating day when he was arrested and exposed as a fraud, my fear crept back, but as soon as we discovered Zoe Jennings with the drone control in her hand, I relaxed again. Right now, I don't know what I think. Lady Dulvington asked me if I'd like to paint the ruins, but I've no idea how I'd feel once I was there. I have booked into an art class, though. I've always wanted to take up art as a hobby, and she's given me the encouragement to make a start."

"At least Alnchurch Park will be in safe hands," I said. "There's an enormous amount of affection between Lady Dulvington and Zoe. I'm not surprised, given the circumstances around her own birth mother's death. It must be absolutely devastating to carry a baby, and then have it taken from you against your will. No wonder her mother killed herself."

"Preservation of history is very important," said Oscar. "Even if it rhymes. But I think all this paranormal investigating is taking its toll on me. I'm starting to imagine things. When we left Lady Dulvington's the other night, you had your car roof open, didn't you, Emily?"

"Yep. I always do. What's the point in having a convertible if you don't convert it?"

"Hmm. As we pulled out of her drive, I thought I heard footsteps in the road. The moon was out, but I couldn't see anyone. Did either of you two hear a scrunch-scrunch-scrunch approaching us, circling around in the lane from the direction of the windmill?"

"I didn't," I said. "Did you, Emily?"

"No, but I was focussing on the task of driving up that steep hill."

"It must've been my imagination," said Oscar. "That's the only explanation. This entire series of events has confirmed my belief that there's no such thing as ghosts."

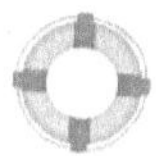

"Shiraz, d'you promise they won't know it's me? I'm more scared of this than any ghost." Emily teetered on black Jimmy Choo platform heels. She wore a full-length, red, Jean Paul Gaultier dress which, without the tall shoes, would've been far too long for her, and a wide-brimmed Philip Treacy hat which partly covered her face. Together with a dark wig I'd found and a pair of Dolce and Gabbana sunglasses, nobody in the audience was ever going to recognise her. Potential bidders filled the hall, as people from Redcliff, Alnchurch, Headland Bay and Brighthaven gawped at designer outfits which they'd only ever seen before on the television.

"Of course they won't know it's you," I said. "Oscar's going to announce you as a special guest. Are you ready?"

"As ready as I'll ever be. How do people walk in these shoes?"

"Carefully," I replied. "Okay, stand by. Here we go." I watched as Oscar grabbed the microphone, and the crowd assembled in Redcliff Community Hall quietened.

"Thank you very much for coming tonight, everyone," said Oscar's voice through the speakers. "I'm honoured to have been your compere at the first ever Redcliff Marine Rescue Fashion Show, and I'm pleased to announce the bids on the outfits you've witnessed so far tonight have raised nine thousand pounds. Together with the anonymous donation of ten thousand pounds, we almost have enough money to buy Redcliff Marine Rescue the vital piece of equipment which the crew needs to keep everyone safe at sea."

Applause and whoops spread around the assembled crowd.

"However…" He raised his voice and waved his hand to signal for quiet. "However, we still need another one thousand pounds to reach our target. And we have one more outfit to show you. But, this time, it won't be our wonderful ex-model, marine rescue volunteer, Shiraz, posing for you. No, indeed. Tonight, ladies and gentlemen, for your entertainment and to encourage you to put your hands in your pockets for one last time, Shiraz has invited her friend, a world-famous supermodel, to Redcliff-upon-Sea."

I peeked around the curtain as the audience murmured amongst themselves.

"I can't do it, Shiraz," said Emily. She bit her lip, as her makeup glowed under the stage lights.

"Yes, you can." I handed her a Champagne flute. "Here, have a second glass of Bollinger. Just don't tip off those heels."

"Are we ready, Redcliff?" said Oscar's voice. "A world-famous supermodel, all the way from Milan, ladies and gentlemen, please put your hands together for the great Emiliana Philpottini."

The crowd clapped and cheered as I desperately tried not to squirt Champagne down my nose. Oscar and I had failed to conclude our discussion on how he should announce Emily, and I wondered how long he'd taken to come up with that fake-Italian mish-mash. I grinned, shoved Emily forwards, and she wobbled down the row of tables we'd assembled to make a catwalk.

"Who'll start the bidding for this"—Oscar scanned his notes—"stunning, unique, red Jean Paul Gaultier dress at five hundred pounds? Thank you, Madam. Six hundred? Do we have six hundred? Thank you, Sir. Seven hundred? The bid is with you, sir, at seven hundred. Any advance on seven hundred? Anyone? Come on, ladies and gentlemen; we need one thousand pounds. A Jean Paul Gaultier dress, complete with a"—he glanced at his notes again—"Philip Treacy hat and Dolce and Gabbana sunglasses. This outfit would usually cost thousands. Tens of thousands. Admire this stunning dress, modelled by our special guest, Emiliana Philpottini, flown here at great expense from Milan. One thousand pounds needed only. The bid is with you, Madam. Could you give me another hundred? Are you out, sir?"

Emily strutted to the end of the catwalk and struck a pose I'd taught her that afternoon. I held my breath and desperately hoped she wouldn't tumble backwards off her shoes, like I'd done once as part of a publicity stunt.

"Is that it?" called Oscar into the microphone. "Are we all done? Wait, do we have a bid from the back of the room?"

The crowd's necks swivelled to stare. I couldn't see past the assembled throng, but thankfully Oscar could.

"Do I hear one thousand pounds?" he said. "One thousand pounds. The bid is with the lady at the rear of the hall. Are we all done? Are we finished? At one thousand pounds, going, going, gone."

Oscar slammed down his rolled-up newspaper, and the crowd burst into more applause. I peeked around the curtain to see who'd made the winning bid, but people getting up and preparing to leave obscured my view.

"We did it," I said to Murph, as he pushed his way to the front and clambered onto the stage to join me. "We reached our target. Now we can replace the broken FLIR."

"Well done, Shiraz. I'll order it tomorrow. It'll be great to have our equipment fully operational again."

"By the way," I said. "You were standing near the back. Did you happen to notice who made the winning bid for that last dress?"

"Yes. An older lady, very elegant, with a younger woman, holding the leads of three small dogs. I don't know her, but she told me she'd wear it to the Marine Rescue Christmas Ball." He lowered his voice. "Don't tell Emily, but I knew it was her in the dress. She played her part beautifully. You're an excellent teacher, Shiraz."

"And so are you, Murph. I'm looking forward to learning more from you and earning my qualified crew certification."

"Excellent. As soon as the new FLIR's fitted, I want to get all you recruits signed off on night searches. By now, you're well practised at searching after dark."

I grinned at him and returned backstage, where Emily would definitely need my help unzipping herself out of Lady Dulvington's new outfit.

THE END

SHIRAZ'S NEXT ADVENTURE

Hi, it's Simon.

Thank you so much for reading *A Spook in the Dark at Alnchurch Park*, the fifth in my *Shiraz Jones Marine Rescue Mysteries* series.

Shiraz, Emily and Oscar will get into more scrapes soon, and in the meantime, if you'd like to learn more about the story behind Shiraz's adventures in Redcliff, why not:

Sign up for my monthly newsletter at simonmichaelprior.com, where we chat about life in Australia, see photos of my work in marine rescue, share a first look at new covers and find out about new releases.

Follow me on Amazon to be notified of new releases by clicking here: Author page (US)

And please consider leaving a review to let other readers know how much you enjoyed it. A few words will suffice. Even if you didn't buy the book from Amazon, you can still leave a review there if you have a valid Amazon account. I read every one with interest and gratitude.

MORE BOOKS BY SIMON

Available on Amazon and from all good bookshops

Shiraz Jones Marine Rescue Mysteries

A Murderous Clamour at Redcliff Manor
A Deadly Affair in the Pirate's Lair
A Landslide, a Bride and a Fatal Ride
A Smuggler's Cave and a Watery Grave
A Spook in the Dark at Alnchurch Park

Fun Travel Memoirs

The Coconut Wireless:
A Travel Adventure in Search of the Queen of Tonga

The Scenicland Radio:
A Travel Adventure in Search of the New Zealand Experience

The Pomegranate Busker:
A Travel Adventure in Search of New Zealand Rock Stardom

The Anticlockwise Proposal:
A Travel Adventure Around the World in Eighty Diamonds

A Capybara for Christmas:
European Travel, Japanese Adventure, Maximum Mayhem

Historical Memoirs

An Englishman in New York:
The Memoirs of John Miskin Prior 1948-1949

DISCLAIMER

A Spook in the Dark at Alnchurch Park is a work of fiction, based on the experiences of Simon Michael Prior, a search and rescue skipper with one of the many volunteer marine rescue organisations which seafarers depend on.

Although the book is set in England, the town of Redcliff-upon-Sea, the village of Alnchurch and the surrounding locations are fictional. Alnchurch Park is a fictional ruined house, although, sadly, many old buildings in England suffered the same fate. Redcliff Marine Rescue is a fictional organisation. Montague Jones PR Ltd is a fictional company. *Red Carpet Superstars* magazine is a fictional publication, as is *Country Lady* magazine. Which is a shame, as they sound like dentists' waiting rooms could benefit from their back copies.

Names, characters, places and incidents are either products of the author's imagination or are used fictitiously. Any resemblance to actual events or locales or persons, living or dead, is entirely coincidental.

I had to say that.

ACKNOWLEDGEMENTS

This book wouldn't have been possible without the help of the following people: The wonderful beta readers: Alyson Sheldrake, Dawne Archer, Lisa Rose Wright, Louise Pierce, Rebecca Hislop and Val Poore; your feedback improved the final result so much.

Thank you to Victoria Twead, Matthew J Holmes, Meg LaTorre, Craig Martelle, Angela Ackerman, Becca Puglisi, David Gaughran and Dave Chesson for informative courses, tips and useful tools.

Thank you to Jeff Bezos, for giving independent authors a platform on which to publish our writing.

And thank you so much to the skippers and crew of the AVCGA Volunteer Coastguard. I couldn't have done it without you.

ABOUT THE AUTHOR

Simon Michael Prior experiences constant adventures, hazards and exciting situations as a marine rescue skipper and a commander of rescue operations.

Although Simon is absolutely nothing like Murph, Redcliff Marine Rescue's burly, grumpy coxswain, many of the scenes in his stories are inspired by events he encounters during his duties.

Simon has also lived on two boats and sunk one of them; sold houses, street signs, Indian food and paper bags for a living; visited almost fifty countries and lived in three; qualified as a scuba diving instructor; nearly killed himself learning to wakeboard and built his own house without the benefit of an instruction manual.

He now lives in it by the sea with his wife and twin daughters, where he spends his time regurgitating his experiences on paper before he has so many more that he forgets them.

Website and newsletter sign up: simonmichaelprior.com
Email: simon@simonmichaelprior.com
Facebook: @simonmichaelprior
Instagram: @simonmichaelprior

www.ingramcontent.com/pod-product-compliance
Lightning Source LLC
Chambersburg PA
CBHW030922210726
48290CB00007B/2026